Helen Lillie's tale of life and love in 18th century Scotland takes up in this new novel where her much praised *Home to Strathblane* left off.

Tragic and unforeseen circumstances in the Blane valley see the action centre on the much respected character of the local doctor, Douglas Stewart. The headstrong yet principled son of a Borders manse continues to tangle with the existing order.

Like many Scotsmen before and since, troubled by their time and place in the homeland, the New World beckons.

Helen Lillie grew up in Strathblane. After graduating from Glasgow University where she majored in Scottish History, she went to America to study at the Yale Drama School. For many years she has written a Washington letter for *The Herald* in Glasgow. She and her Scottish husband live in Washington D.C. She has published three other novels and many articles.

STRATHBLANE
AND
AWAY

HELEN LILLIE

Argyll
publishing

© Helen Lillie

First published 1996
Argyll Publishing
Glendaruel
Argyll PA22 3AE
Scotland

**British Library Cataloguing-in-Publication Data.
A catalogue record for this book is available from
the British Library.**

ISBN 1 874640 47 5

Typeset and origination by
Cordfall Ltd, Civic Street, Glasgow
Printed and bound in Great Britain by
Cromwell Press, Wiltshire

Fondly dedicated
to my husband,
Charles Robert Scott Marwick,
and in memory of my mother,
Helen Barbara Lillie,
whose ashes lie in Melrose Abbey

ACKNOWLEDGEMENTS

The readers of *Home to Strathblane* who asked me what happened to my characters are responsible for this book. And many of the individuals who gave me guidance then also contributed to this sequel, in particular my cousin Dr Morag L Insley who drove me round the Scottish Borders to refresh my memories of where my mother's ancestors came from. My late uncle Sheriff John A Little QC LLD and my granduncle Adam Tait of Wooplaw were responsible for my interest in Border lore.

According to their tombstones in Melrose Abbey, the Tait family lived in Darnick from the seventeenth century and as Prebyterians they'd have "sat under" the Reverend Thomas Stewart if he and his church and manse had ever existed outside of my imagination. I have taken the liberty of building a completely fictitious nineteenth century Darnick so topographical errors are mine alone.

In addition I offer thanks to my publisher Derek Rodger for his contructive editing, my agent Cathie Thomson, Anne Johnston of *The Herald* who lives in the Blane Valley, Miss Helen Lowe CA whose office is on Charlotte Square in Edinburgh, my critic and reinforcer

Sylvia Sunderlin of Washington DC, Dr Catherine Gavin my continuing role-model, the choir of the Georgetown Presbyterian Church in Washington for musical help, and my husband Charles Scott Marwick for his invaluable practical assistance on the manuscript.

Helen Lillie
Washington DC
September 1995

CONTENTS

PART ONE

CHANGES

"Any man's death diminishes me, because I am involved in mankind; and therefore never send to know for whom the bell tolls; it tolls for thee."

John Donne (1571–1631)
Devotions

I

One death diminishes us all, as the poet Donne says. And it changes the course of lives left behind.

The future of two Scottish families, the Stewarts and the Patersons who lived in Stirlingshire's beautiful Blane Valley, veered off in different directions after Primrose Paterson died in childbirth in the Spring of 1802.

She had been warned by her physician, Doctor Douglas Stewart, and by specialists in the nearby city of Glasgow to whom he had sent her, that she must never have another baby after the dreadful labours which produced her two daughters, Mary and Anne.

But in her short life, Primrose had always got her own way. Wellborn and beautiful, she had picked out her own husband, no small achievement in the Eighteenth Century when arranged marriages were customary. Walter Paterson had not been rich when they first met, but the couple had been happy and had prospered through his cultivation of a small estate named Leddrie Green in the parish of Strathblane.

But every woman, in 1802, was expected to provide a male heir to inherit property. Otherwise, she had failed as a helpmeet.

So Primrose disregarded her physicians' advice. She became pregnant again and she died, as they said she would. Dr Stewart gave her the best of care, treated her according to the recommended medical practices of the time, dieted her, bled her regularly, made her rest. But it wasn't enough.

At least she survived long enough to know that she had accomplished what she had set out to do.

"It *is* a boy. A strong healthy one." The doctor told her, and as her maid, Mamie MacLean, took the baby away to wash it, Primrose had let her life go, the start of a smile on her beautiful face.

Douglas Stewart was not a religious man and Strathblane was a Presbyterian parish, but as he closed her eyes he sang very softly over the dead woman the melody of the "Rest ye calmly" chorus from Bach's St Matthew's Passion. It had been a favourite of hers. Then, with a release of emotion he rarely allowed himself in a professional setting, he kissed the hands that would never play the piano again.

Primrose had been far more to him than a patient. Ten years before, in 1792, he had arrived in Strathblane from Edinburgh, forced out of a promising medical career by the turbulent political climate. His first friend in the Blane Valley had been Walter Paterson, whom he had treated successfully for serious injuries, mental as well as physical, which the young man had suffered during his escape from Revolutionary France.

And, while he was wooing his own wife, Jean, a farmer's daughter, Douglas Stewart had played a small but important part in expediting the romance of his handsome patient with Primrose Moncrieff, whose brother was the influential Laird of Kirklands.

So the destinies of the two couples, married in the same year, 1793, had been interlinked, although their daily lives had progressed in opposite directions. Walter Paterson, a banker's son from a happy, well-connected Edinburgh family, had a good head for business. He also had literary gifts and had published several collections of essays and poetry. He had grown up in France among members of the *ancien regime* and had been quickly accepted by the Blane Valley's gentry when he married Primrose and settled down in Leddrie Green House.

Although his skill was widely sought throughout the Blane Valley, the able ambitious Douglas Stewart, the eldest son of a dour Border manse, had remained an impecunious country doctor. With a growing family to support, he and his wife did little socializing, and his only relaxation was singing. Primrose Paterson, impressed by the quality of his fine baritone voice, had taught him how to read music so that he could join a small group in Strathblane which studied the classic works of Bach and Handel and the modern operas of Mozart. This had opened up a whole new emotional outlet to the young man and for it he would forever be indebted to the woman who had just died.

During the last stage of the fatal delivery, the doctor had sent an urgent message to his home across the valley, asking his wife to come to Leddrie Green House. Jean Stewart had nursed Walter Paterson when he had first arrived in Strathblane and their relationship was more like that of a mother and child than of contemporaries.

So, when her husband broke the tragic news to his friend, she was there to gather the distraught widower in her arms, support him through his first storm of grief and eventually persuade him to drink a posset heavily laced with laudanum.

Mrs Moncrieff, the Laird's wife, had also hastened to Leddrie Green when she heard that her sister-in-law was in labour. A warm, capable woman, with three children of her own, she had whisked the two little Paterson daughters, Mary and Anne, over to Kirklands House, then returned.

"Thank goodness Henry's away at the horse fair in Stirling," Alison Moncrieff said frankly to the Stewarts after she and Jean had put the sedated Walter to bed. "The poor man couldn't have done anything and he'd be out of his mind, he so adored his little sister. I'll have the children brought back here and I'll stay on to help with the funeral arrangements and try to console poor Walter. I know what he's going through. I was widowed once myself. And how fortunate," she added, "that Mamie MacLean's just had another child and can act as wet nurse to the baby."

An understanding woman, she now turned to Douglas, taking his hands in hers. "I know you feel terrible. But you'd warned them both often enough. You must never blame yourself."

Her sympathy almost broke through the exhausted doctor's control. Hoarsely he told her, "Send for me at once when the drug starts to wear off. And if there's anything you can think of that I can do for him or for the children, anything at all, Mrs Moncrieff. . ."

"I will," she assured him. "But now it's late and they're bringing your horse around from the stable. Go home. You need rest and remember that everyone in the parish needs *you*."

When Douglas had mounted the plodding old mare, a footman hoisted Jean up behind him and they rode off down the long drive and across the Blane Valley. As they passed the Strathblane Church she asked, "Should we stop off at the manse and tell the minister?"

"No," he answered. "Paterson's asleep. He doesna need company the now. By morn Mr Gardner will have heard. Like everyone else in the parish. And Jeannie, I've had enough. I want to go home."

As they reached Blaerisk, their own little house, its backdoor burst open and their two small sons rushed out. The doctor patted their heads absently, stabled the horse, then made straight for the dining room sideboard, where he picked up a whisky decanter and a glass, then disappeared upstairs to his bedroom.

His wife gave the horse its fodder, then hustled her brood into the kitchen where Mrs MacGregor, the elderly housekeeper, was giving Meg, the youngest child, a bottle.

"Ye're a' to stay down here and be quiet," Jean ordered. "Yer father's gey tired." She took a deep breath. "There's a new wee son at Leddrie Green. But ye're no to ask him about it. . ."

"Why not?" demanded Angus, a formidable nine-year-old who showed signs of growing up to be a big man like his father.

"Because . . . Mrs Paterson's gone to Heaven. . ." She looked at Mrs MacGregor, who gasped.

"Is she wi God?" pursued Angus.

Jean swallowed. "Aye. I . . . suppose so. . ."

"Do ye mean she's dead?" asked Tommy, their second son, who had a literal mind. When she nodded, he surprised her by running to her and pressing her quivering hand, as his father did when comforting a patient.

The tears Jean had been holding back gushed out. "Aye. She's dead. And . . . naething will ever be the same." She pulled off her shawl and bonnet so violently her heavy dark hair came loose and tumbled down her back. Although she was careful of her appearance and her few good clothes, she paid no heed to them now.

"Gang up to the doctor, Ma'am," said the housekeeper. "I'll put the bairns to bed. Tell him there's a pot o' soup on the stove."

Jean knew he would not want food, but she mumbled a heartfelt "Thank ye," kissed her children goodnight and managed to reach the bedroom before her sobbing was beyond control. Snecking the latch on the door, she threw herself on top of her husband, who lay, still dressed, on the bed. He held her tightly. Though he was dry-eyed she felt the grief in him.

"Ye want a dram, Jeannie?"

She shook her head. "Will the bairn live?"

"Aye. Most like. It's a big, strapping child. I should never have let her carry it to term."

"But she wanted a son awful bad! And ye've no cause to blame yersel. Ye telt them she was to have no more, after Anne was born, six years back."

"Aye. I did warn both of them she couldna go through that again."

"But she twisted him around her wee fingers, persuaded him she'd be a' right. . . Did she . . . know?"

"Aye. She was far gone but I think she understood when I telt her." He remembered the brief smile. "But what'll happen to Paterson now? He's no but thirty and a' the poetry and music in the world willna comfort him."

"He'll marry again."

"Never. No after the way he idolized her."

"Ma auntie aye said it was the men that was the maist inconsolable that took anither wife the fastest."

"Auntie Semple was usually right, but I dinna foresee it in this case."

Jean's aunt, long dead, had been the midwife in Strathblane when Douglas Stewart arrived there and they had greatly respected each other.

The couple lay close, as they always did. When Jean's tears stopped, she got up, undressed, and drew on a voluminous white cotton nightgown. Then she unlaced her husband's boots. One was heavily reinforced with metal and leather bands, for he had a crippled left foot, and this she massaged briefly, as she did each night. She started to unbutton his shirt, but with an effort he pushed himself up in the bed and dragged it off, followed by his breeches and heavy white stockings. She handed him a nightshirt and gathered his daytime clothes up from the floor.

But as she turned towards the door, he caught her arm. "Jeannie. Stay wi me. I maun talk or I'll go mad."

"I'm just takin' these down to soak." They were stained with blood. "It's yer guid suit and ye maun be ready to gang up to Kirklands when the Laird comes home and hears the news."

The doctor groaned. "Aye. He'll hae a gastric attack for sure."

When she came back, after fending off more questions from Angus and Tommy and telling them to remember Mary and Anne in their prayers, she found that her husband had pulled a plaid up around his shoulders which he did when very tired. He was a big, powerfully built man, distinguished looking rather than handsome, with short, springy dark hair turning prematurely grey at the temples. She thought he was asleep but, when she lay down beside him, she knew he was wide awake.

He was not reliving the tragic day. He had done his best and accepted the outcome. But Primrose's death was a personal loss so strong that, manlike, he could only cope with it by turning his mind onto something else.

"Jeannie. I'm gettin' on. I'll be thirty-four on my next birthday."

"That's no so old, these days, Dougie. If ye're weary, it's because ye were up all last night and ye've had little to eat for mony hours."

"That's no what I mean. I've been a country doctor for ten years. I've made no advancement in my profession."

"Ye have too, Dougie. Ye've a big practice nowadays. The gentry in the Valley are no goin' to Glasgow for their surgery. They're sending for you. And Dr Ogilvy in Killearn is aye callin' ye in on cases he canna manage."

"Aye, because I'm an unusually successful surgeon. I should be doing more operating."

She waited. Marriage had taught her to be silent when he was in these moods.

"Jock MacLean'll be coming back soon from Edinburgh wi his degree from the Medical College. He'll no be my apprentice any more. He'd have graduated last year, if it hadna been for that skulduggery among the examiners. My old enemy David Baxter that heard I was helpin' to pay for his education. . ."

"Oh Dougie! Dougie! Leave that subject be! Ye'll never prove anything!"

"Maybe not. But my auld chief, Dr Tait, as guid as telt me when he wrote and said he'd make sure Jock qualified this year. I've aye telt the laddie I'd turn the practice over to him once he was trained."

"There's enough patients nowadays for the two of you."

"I don't think so."

"The parish has far more people now than when he went away . . . near eight hundred, the minister telt me."

"Aye, but the factory that made the inkle cloth is closing down. It lost that much trade during the long war with France."

"Dougie, we're at peace now and new mills are opening in Campsie Glen. They're hiring weavers from Renfrewshire, and there's workers flocking down from the Highlands into the Valley. The Kirk Session's talking about takin' on an extra dominie, there's that many bairns in the school. Ye mind, when ye engrafted them last against the smallpox, it took ye twice as long."

"Aye. Because Jock wasna there to assist me." He sighed. "And there'll be a big difference, Jeannie, when Jock comes back. As my apprentice, I just gave him room and board and let him keep any money the patients handed him, when he bled them or the like. But now he's a doctor himself and wi a family to support. And Jeannie . . . it's no just that."

He could not bear to face Walter Paterson whose adored wife he had failed to save. But he wasn't ready to admit it yet. Instead, he reached for the whisky.

Then, deliberately, he put the bottle down untouched. "No. I've had one already. I'm startin' to drink too much. Because I'm tired and stale. The only professional stimulus I get are visits to Glasgow for lectures, and half the time I'm giving them masel, on ma work with the public health, the engrafting."

His voice rose. "Apart from that, a' I do here is treat sniffles and coughs and rheumatics . . . and confinements. Maybe there's some new procedure in obstetrics that I dinna know about. I try to keep up wi what's happening in medicine but I canna. Maybe if I'd had more knowledge I could have saved her. I want to go away from here!" he blurted out. "I want to leave Strathblane, live in a city again, where I can move on up in ma profession, make more money, have a better life!"

"Dougie! Whaur would ye go?" She was alarmed. He had raised this subject before but he had never been so vehement about it.

"Maybe back to Edinburgh. Or to London. Or even overseas to America. . . "

"Ye canna put the clock back, Dougie. It wouldna be the way it was when ye were a student, goin' to plays every night." And making love to actresses, she added silently.

"I didna go to the theatre every night. And ma interests are different nowadays. I prefer music."

"Aye. And ye're a married man wi three bairns to support."

"Wi more to come, most likely," he added proph-
etically.

For later, that night, when Jean had distracted him in
the way she had found most effective, their next child was
conceived, the first of the many changes in their lives
resulting from Primrose Paterson's death.

II

Walter Paterson's grief dominated his whole life. During
the day, he had, perforce, to keep it under control, for his
estate needed constant supervision. He also had literary
commitments and his Edinburgh publisher was expecting
delivery of a collection of essays. But these Walter had to
set aside, for he could not write or even revise. Primrose
had been his inspiration and she had always copied and
edited his manuscripts, for he trusted her literary judgment.

Walter had many friends in the Blane Valley, but now
he couldn't bear to see them. Nor could he bring himself
to go up to Kirklands House where his brother-in-law's
grief matched his own.

The only house Walter felt like visiting, during the
long, light, spring evenings, was the Stewarts' bustling little
establishment, Blaerisk. There Jean did her best to make
him take some nourishment and the doctor, if he was home,
would try to start a stimulating argument which salved his
own sore spirit.

Walter was present therefore, one late afternoon when
Strathblane's elderly parish minister, Mr Gardner, also
came to call.

"I am glad to find ye at home, Douglas," said he. In
private he called the doctor by his first name for they were
close friends. Sitting down and accepting a cup of tea, he

continued, "I have a letter to deliver to you from your father in the Borders. He is still the pastor in Darnick, where I wrote to him, you may recall, at the time of your marriage, in an attempt to heal the breach between you."

"Aye." The doctor had had a long, dreary day and felt low. "And he never had the courtesy to send you a reply."

"True," said Mr Gardner equably, "but seemingly he kept my letter. And he wishes to see you now." He drew some papers from his pocket and handed them over.

Douglas unfolded the communications, glanced at them, then read aloud in his fine resonant voice:

> *Dear Mr Gardner:*
>
> *Circumstances require that I find my son, Douglas. The last word I had of him was a letter from your good self, written in March, 1793, when you performed his marriage service. If he still resides in your parish, I would appreciate your giving him the enclosed letter. If he has moved, and you know his whereabouts, perhaps you would be so kind as to redirect it, or advise me where and how I may find him. I continue to be pastor of Darnick Parish, which lies close to the town of Melrose.*
>
> *The matter is of some urgency otherwise I would not importune you.*
>
> *Trusting that you and yours enjoy good health, I am, your colleague in the Work of the Lord,*
> *Thomas Stewart*

Douglas tossed this note onto the table and read out the enclosure:

> *Dear Son,*
> *Your mother is mortally ill and desires so vehemently to see you that I am prepared to*

forget the past and allow you to return home.
You must do this as soon as you can, and bring
your wife and any children you may have sired.
There is plenty of room in the Manse since only
your sister Jennifer now remains with us.
In the sad circumstances it is Christian duty to
set aside our differences.
You may write and advise me when to expect
your arrival and how many will accompany
you. To ignore this letter could lie heavily on
your conscience if you retain any filial feelings
for the woman who gave you life and who,
despite your neglect of her these many years,
has not forgotten you.
T Stewart

"The auld hypocrite! As if the breach was my fault! *He* may be able to forget the past and . . . what's that he said? . . . *set aside our differences* . . . but it's no that easy for me!"

Douglas tossed down the letters on the table, as the anger poured out of him. "He threw me out of ma home without even ma few possessions! And a' because I cam' back from the University in Edinburgh and tried to explain to him I'd no call for divinity. I wanted to help humanity studying medicine. But no! He wouldna listen! Just shouted and yelled and slammed the door. And me no but a young laddie. I could have starved to death, and I near did."

"Your quarrel was with your father and not your mother," said Mr Gardner.

"That's true."

"Did you ever try to get in touch with her?"

"Aye. When I won the first of my prizes at the Medical College. But that was before we had the penny post and I'm thinking the old man never accepted the letter, for I got no answer. It would have been like him, to refuse to pay for it, when he saw my handwriting on the cover."

"And does he no realise ye've responsibilities here . . . wi yer practice and family?" Jean interposed.

"A fat lot he cares, the auld bastard. . ."

The minister held up his hands. "Your anger is understandable, Douglas, but I think you should read these two letters again. As I see it, your father has humbled his pride because your mother is dying. How old would she be?"

"In her seventies, at least. And she was never strong. She had several stillbirths after the four of us were born."

"You were the eldest?"

"Aye, and her favourite." He seldom thought of his youth but now the memories came rushing back. "I had more sympathy with her sicknesses than the rest o' the family. I'd had so much pain masel when I had the fever that crippled my foot. I used to come home from school and rub her back, sing to her, try to cheer her up when she was poorly. . ." He stopped, clearing his throat.

"And now she needs ye again, Dougie," said Jean. "And she wants to see her grandchildren afore she dies. I think we should gang to Darnick."

"Are ye crazy, woman? How could I transport you and three wee bairns half way across Scotland?"

"I can solve that problem," said Walter Paterson. "You go in that beautiful roomy carriage I bought for Primrose. No-one needs it now."

"It's far too big for me to handle. Wi two horses on unfamiliar roads, I'd overturn it and kill us all."

"You could take Rabb Innes. I've little use for a coachman nowadays. And a trip would do him good, he's grieving for her, too. He misses the jaunts into town. And he knows the best routes to Edinburgh, where to break your journey. And when you get to the Capital," Walter went on, in a brief upsurge of enthusiasm," you can stay with my sister Clementina. Her husband's gone to Paris to see his parents, now there's peace with France."

Walter's other brother-in-law, the Vicomte de Sincerbeaux, had lived in Scotland since the Reign of Terror.

"Did Clemmie no go with him?" asked Jean.

"She found she was *enceinte* again. And Louis's family never did think she was good enough for him because she was a banker's daughter. But he's taken little Armand, who's the heir to the title and the Sincerbeaux estates. If there are any left, since the Revolution."

"You would certainly have to break the journey in Edinburgh," put in Mr Gardner. "And maybe you could stop over for a day and see some of your old friends there, Douglas."

"That should be an inducement for you," added Walter Paterson.

"But ye're talking as if this could a' be arranged!" The doctor stood up and started pacing the floor, his habit when troubled. "What about ma practice here? Ma patients?" As if on cue, the tirling pin on the front door rasped loudly and Mrs MacGregor ushered in a distraught little boy.

"Doctor! Ma mammie needs ye quick! She's haein' pains awfu' close, she thinks the bairn's comin'!"

Douglas reached for his bag. "Run and tell her I'm right behind ye! Who's with her?"

"Naebody! It cam on that unexpected. Ma faither's at the cattle fair and ma granny's gone to Drymen to ma auntie there."

"Aweel, go tell her I'm coming! I'm just makin' sure I hae a' I'll need."

"And I'll be over later to gie ye supper and help," added Jean.

As the child ran out the doctor turned to his friends. "Ye see? An emergency. No time to fetch Dr Ogilvy. Effie McLaren's no an alarmist. If she says she needs me in a hurry, she does indeed. She's had premature labours afore." He was pushing a case with forceps and other instruments into his bag. "And there's no midwife in Strathblane, now Jean's auntie's dead." He turned to the minister. "I ken I should go to my mother but I hae responsibilities of ma own. I'm the only doctor for many miles around."

III

A few days later, that situation changed. As Jean from her bedroom window watched the stagecoach from Glasgow inch its way carefully down the steep brae to the village, there was a thunderous pounding on the front door and when she rushed to open it, she found a travel-stained but cheerful young man on the stoup, surrounded by bundles.

"Jock!" She threw her arms around him. "Eh! Laddie, ye're back frae Edinburgh!"

"Aye! And although you and your guid man may continue to address me as Jock, to the rest of the parish I am now . . ." he struck a pose . . . "*Doctor* John MacLean wi a string o' letters after ma name to prove it!"

Mrs MacGregor emerged from the kitchen and also enveloped him in her arms. "And jist in time to help out here!"

"Why? What's happened? And where's my wife? Where's Mamie?"

"She's at Leddrie Green wi her baby. She's wet nurse

for Mrs Paterson's wee son. Oh Jock! Did ye hear about the tragedy?" Jean's tears started.

"Aye. When I changed coaches in Glasgow I met Geordie from Kirklands and he telt me the Laird was terrible upset. The doctor maun be hard hit, too, though no surprised, I fear. Where is he?"

"Off up the Boards Road someplace. Gang on over to Leddrie Green and bring Mamie back wi ye for dinner. Oh Jock! Dougie'll be that pleased ye got yer degree!"

"I've a lot to tell him about how that finally came to pass . . . and here he is the now!"

For Douglas had just come through the front door, his tired face lighting up when he saw who was there.

"Jock! Or should I say . . . Doctor MacLean?"

"You should indeed, sir! And it's a' your doing!"

"You did a' the studyin', laddie. I just put up some o' the money. And ye've qualified in the nick of time for I'm makin' a trip to the Borders, leavin' you in charge o' the practice!"

Jock's face fell. "Oh no! I couldna do that!"

"What for no'? Ye did it afore, when I was sick. Ye even treated me, masel. And ye werena trained in those days!"

Jock grinned. "Aye. I didna realise how little I knew!"

"Aweel, ye do now. And ye can ask Dr Ogilvy up the Valley, if ye need advice. A nice man and ye know him well."

Jean looked at her husband. "So we're really going?"

He shrugged his shoulders. "Why not?"

A couple of days later, when he had completed his rounds, Douglas stopped by the Manse and as he had hoped, found the minister alone.

"Mr Gardner, I'll no beat about the bush. I need you

to write to my father and tell him we're coming to Darnick."

"I'm surprised that you have not already written to him yourself."

The doctor looked down at his hands. He had a habit of flexing and kneading his long, sensitive fingers when pondering. Now he was studying them as though seeking for himself the reassurance their touch so often gave to his patients.

"I've tried to write and I canna do it. I'm ashamed to admit this to a man of your cloth, but . . . I'm ower full of old resentments."

"That is understandable. You were young and raw when he disowned you. But maybe the time has come for reconciliation. For both of you. You seldom speak of your father. What manner of man is he?"

Douglas considered the question. "He was – probably still is – a greatly admired preacher and a popular pastor, widely known for his learning and his social grace. But in his home he's a domestic tyrant. He demanded unquestioning obedience from us children and to get it, he'd beat us, or shout and yell. I never wanted to be a minister but when he packed me off to study divinity, I was too scared to disobey. Then, after a year in Edinburgh, I found I couldna go through wi it."

He had discovered he was an agnostic, though he would never admit this to Mr Gardner.

"You had grown in self-knowledge and knew you would do more good as a physician. Did you not explain this to him?"

"I tried but he wouldna listen. He just raged like a mad bull and tossed me bodily out of the Manse, telt me never to come back, not even to say goodbye to my mother and ma sister and brothers."

"What did you do?"

"It was late at night, I remember. And cold. I went to the doctor's house. He'd taught me to how to walk after I was lamed, encouraged ma interest in medicine. . . And he knew ma father for what he was. He believed me when I telt him ma story." Douglas pushed back his thick greying hair. "That man was my idea of a real Christian. He lent me money to go back to Edinburgh and wrote letters of recommendation for me to people he knew. So I was able to attend classes at the Medical College and find work at the Infirmary and with private physicians to support myself. I walked on at the Theatre Royal as an extra too, though I found that job on ma own."

"Is this worthy man still alive?"

"No. He died nine years ago. He'd kept me in touch with my mother, but since then . . . I've heard nothing from Darnick. "He flexed his fingers again. "It's as if my father had slaughtered me like a farm animal."

"Well, now he seeks to resurrect you."

"Aye, but without either understanding or forgiveness. That letter! Did you ever read such chopped sentences? He's a scholar. He expresses himself well on paper, but when he had to write and ask me to come home, it stuck in his craw."

"Possibly he was embarrassed."

"And so he should be. I hope I never treat *my* sons that way."

The minister nodded but kept silent, knowing there was more to come.

"Mr Gardner, what he said I can never forget even though I realise it came out in the heat of the moment. He telt me I was rotten through and through and I'd never amount to onything."

"Well, you have proved him to be wrong. You are one of the most respected physicians in the West. The

University of Glasgow has asked you to lecture. Your
patients come from far and wide." He smiled. "And you
know yourself what people say in unbridled moments. For
if ye'll forgive me, Douglas, ye've inherited a fair share o'
your father's temper!"

"True." He clenched his hands hard. "But . . . he was
proved correct once. I fell into bad trouble, in Edinburgh.
That's why I came here."

"I was aware of that but never knew what exactly
happened."

"In a drunken brawl I near killed one of my classmates.
David Baxter. A proper bastard who'd aye been jealous o'
my ability for he had little enough of his own. He got
through college on his medical connections. His father was
a surgeon in Fife."

"A student brawl is just a . . . a peccadillo."

"Aye. But that was when the Revolution was under
way in France. People were unco' scared of change. And I
was brought before Judge Braxfield – the Hangin' Judge
they called him. Baxter lied in his teeth, said that I'd been
talking sedition. I could have been hanged or sent to
Australia, like yon Radical fellow, Thomas Muir, if Dr Tait
hadna intervened for me. He's a much respected man in
the Capital and I was his assistant at the time."

There was a long silence. "When your wife nursed
me through the pneumonia, here in the Manse, she must
have seen the scars on my back." Mr Gardner nodded.
"Judge Braxfield sentenced me to a public floggin' wi the
cat o' nine tails." He shivered. "I still have nightmares about
it. And now Davie Baxter's a fashionable physician in
Edinburgh. He examines students, makes sure none get
degrees without proper qualifications. Last year, when he
learned Jock MacLean was my apprentice, he turned in an
adverse report on him, which cost the laddie a year of his

life, and me a lot of money I could ill afford."

"Your father had nothing to do with that."

"I think maybe he had. Darnick's no but forty or fifty miles from Edinburgh. He knows a lot of people. He knew all about my disgrace. And I did do wrong, Mr Gardner."

"Douglas, you were young."

"Aye, young and fou, but that's no excuse. I tried to kill a man and I near did. Me that had taken an oath to do no harm." Douglas stood up. "That's why I canna write to him now. I've tried but words won't come."

"Have you considered addressing the letter to your mother? All you need to say is when you expect to arrive and that you are bringing Jean and the bairns. You might also tell her their names and how old they are."

"Aye. That I could do."

"Then sit ye down here and write just that. And on your way home, you can leave it at the Kirkhouse Inn to be picked up by the mail coach."

Douglas settled himself at the minister's desk, then hesitated. "Mr Gardner . . ."

"Yes?"

"I . . ." Again he ran his hands through his hair. "I'm scared to go back to Edinburgh. To meet up with people who saw ma public punishment. Baxter was there . . . I saw him in the crowd, waitin for the lash to fall on ma back. Every time. And others that I'd thought were my friends."

"Did Jean not tell me you would stay with Mr Paterson's sister in her house on Charlotte Square?"

"Aye. He wrote to her and she sent us the most warm invitation. She's awful fond of Jean. They met when the Sincerbeaux family visited Strathblane. Clementina wants us to stay several days, so they can go shopping. And there's a concert she said I'd enjoy. . ."

Mr Gardner smiled. "And at that concert, Douglas, you would be the house guest of a Viscountess, a far cry from a common criminal."

"True." He picked up one of the minister's pens. "I wish I'd had a father like you, sir."

"And oftentimes I've felt paternally towards you, watching you struggle wi your frustrations here. When you're finished, we'll share a dram unless ye'd prefer tea."

"Ye ken fine I'd prefer a dram. And I'll need one, I'm thinking."

But, to his surprise, the words of the letter came easily.

My dearest Mama,

I look forward to seeing you again very soon. Jean, my wife, and I will leave for Edinburgh within the week, and will break our journey there to rest our three children – Angus aged nine, Thomas aged seven, and Margaret who is three and named after you. We had a stillborn child eighteen months ago for whom my wife still grieves.

Since I cannot give you a precise time for our arrival, we can, if necessary, stay at an inn either in Darnick or Melrose. We are travelling in a private carriage.

I send you my most heartfelt love, and hope that you will be in sufficiently good health and spirits to enjoy your grandchildren who are bonnie bairns.

I am ever your loving son,

Douglas Elliot

At Blaerisk House, Strathblane, Stirlingshire,

May 7, 1802

"An excellent letter," Mr Gardner pronounced." But why did you sign it *Douglas Elliot*?"

"Elliot was my mother's maiden name and she never let me forget I was a Borderer like herself. My father came from Perthshire."

"So you are setting yourself firmly in her camp, in the household."

"Aye, but I promise you I'll do my best to be civil to the old man."

"I will be praying for you."

"I'll remember that."

"It may well be that you'll find your animosity has lost its power over you. People change. You are no longer a boy. Your father is older too."

"I doubt if he's any different."

"He asked you to come home. That was tantamount to an apology. And you have learned to handle calmly a number of unpleasant people here in Strathblane. It has not been easy for you, but I have seen you make progress."

"Thank you," Douglas smiled ruefully. "Mr Gardner, it is ridiculous, I know, for a grown man. But I dread to meet my father. When I was little, he would flog me worse than they did outside the Tolbooth. And he'd be so emotional about it, he aye wanted me to cry wi remorse. Which I never did. . ."

The minister smiled. "He would be unlikely to threaten you physically nowadays, Douglas. And for the rest . . . remember that love casteth out fear. It is your mother you are going to see. You can hold your peace, for her sake."

"Aye. That I know I must do."

PART TWO

THE ROMANTIC TOWN

"Mine own romantic town"
    Sir Walter Scott's description of Edinburgh

I

"It's a mercy Rabb Innes likes children," Douglas remarked to his wife as, for what seemed like the hundredth time, the two little boys demanded that the carriage be halted so that they could stretch their legs, relieve themselves by the roadside, or climb up and sit on the box beside the coachman.

"They're no used to being so cooped up," Jean answered. "They dinna like to sit still for so long."

"Don't they have to sit still in school? I know I did."

"Aye, but then they're busy learning."

"And have I not been telling all about what they'll see in Edinburgh and in the Borders and reading them all those wee books the Paterson children gave them?"

"Ye're just not used having them underfoot a' the time, Dougie." She leaned back in the carriage and closed her eyes. Observing her pale face and the droop of her usually smiling mouth the professional in him noted her weariness. It had been a hectic week of preparation.

She opened her eyes and gave him her sweet smile. "I love them, Dougie. And so do you."

"Aye . . . and I love you, too." When he put his arms around her, she began to cry. "Jeannie! What's wrong?"

"I'm feared I'll disgrace ye afore yer family!"

"How could ye ever do that? They'll see you've been the making of me!"

"I'm no as well educated as you are. Sometimes I

forget and dinna speak proper English."

"So do I. So do we all in Scotland. My mother grew up on a farm, too."

"Aye, but she had schooling, which I never had."

"And who's to know that? Ye're used to associating with gentle people like the Patersons."

"Aye . . . and Clementina will look over my clothes and tell me what to wear. Does yer mother like clothes, Dougie?"

"She did. She aye looked nice. My sister Jenny was still a child when I left home and she was a plain wee Jane."

"Tell me again about yer brothers."

"They were aye more biddable than I was. Kenneth loved the outdoors. He spent a' his time on my uncle's big farm. Alasdair was slow. Maybe the auld man's turned him into the minister he failed to make out of me."

"Angus is fair excited to think that his grandfather is a minister. He's religious, that child."

"So I've observed. D'you suppose we're raising a preacher or a dominie?"

"Ach, he's full o' the De'il too. And the puir wee souls have never had grandparents, wi ma faither and mither both gone before I was married. It's good ye finally hae some time to get to know your family, Dougie. In Strathblane, ye're aye out carin' for ither peoples' bairns."

"Aye, and this is the first time we've been away on a trip wi them, for I recall we left them back at home that time we went to Helensburgh and visited yer cousin Willie."

"Aye, after. . ." She stopped. After she had the stillborn baby. To distract her, he went on, "Ye'll find Edinburgh's a much handsomer city than Glasgow."

She shivered. "But . . . I'll be scared of a' the brilliant people!"

"Clementina will protect you from them, the way you

protected her from the bulls in the Blane Valley!"

He was glad he had reminded her of that because by the time they reached Edinburgh, at the end of two long days of travel, Jean's apprehension was growing.

So, for different reasons, was his own. From the carriage window he pointed out to the children the great hump of the Castle atop the Mound, but he found he could not identify the buildings they were driving past.

"With all these new terraces and streets I'll never find my way around," he complained.

The coachman called down cheerfully, "Never fear, Doctor! The Auld Toon's unchanged. E'en the same dirt on the streets."

When they turned into Charlotte Square and pulled up, Jean gasped.

"Dougie! Is that a' yin house? They Sincerbeaux must be unco' rich!"

"Paterson says they're not as rich as they were before the Revolution. That's why the Viscount studied law here, so he could support his family if need be. Aweel! Here we are. And here's Clementina at the door to welcome us!"

The youthful Vicomtesse de Sincerbeaux was a pretty blond whose sonsy Scottish face, strongly resembling her brother Walter's, contrasted piquantly with her elegant clothes. She was also, Douglas noted, perceptibly pregnant. Her warmth overcame some of Jean's awe at the magnificence of the townhouse. As for the children, they immediately wanted to see the young Sincerbeaux, whom they'd met the year before when they'd visited Strathblane.

"Whaur's Armand?" demanded Angus.

"He's gone to Paris with his Papa to meet his grandparents."

"I'm going to meet my grandparents too!"

"Yes! Isn't it exciting!"

"My grandfather's a minister!"

"Well, well! You'll have to behave yourself. Pierre and Gerard are in bed and you'll be going to bed too! Unless your mother thinks you should have some bread and milk first?"

"Let them have a good run around the house to work off some energy," suggested their father.

Servants were unloading the luggage and carrying it indoors.

"I've put you in the big downstairs bedroom," said the Vicomtesse opening a door, "and the boys can share Armand's room upstairs. There's a little couch in here for Meg."

Jean was looking over her quarters with wide eyes. "That's such a huge fourposter, there'd be room for all of us in it!"

"Oh, but we've lots of space!" said Clementina. "Now come into the morning room and have some refreshment. Just leave your bonnet and shawl, Jean. The maid will put them away for you."

"Oh Clemmie! Ye maun guide me on what I'm to wear!"

"For sure! My seamstress is coming in the morning to let out some of my dresses and she can do anything you need in the way of alterations. . . And Douglas!" She turned her big blue eyes on him. "That wonderful Mozart concert I wrote to you about is tomorrow afternoon and my uncle is having a supper party afterwards."

Her uncle, Lord Paterson, was a judge and presumably would be entertaining friends from the bench. "We really should be pushing on to Darnick," said Douglas.

Jean sank wearily into a chair. "Oh, please, Dougie . . . I maun wash a' the bairns' clothes."

Angus, prancing in after his parents with Tommy at

his heels announced, "We slept at an inn last night and Mama said there were fleas!"

Embarrassed, Jean was quick to reassure her hostess. "Naw! Naw! And if there were, we got rid of them. But . . . I want them to look their best when they meet their granny."

"You're not going to spend your first day in Edinburgh doing laundry! I have a washerwoman and a maid who irons like a dream. And you and I are going shopping. Don't you have things you want to do, Douglas?"

"I should call on Dr Tait. I wrote and told him I was coming to town."

"Oh dear, I hope he's well enough to see you. He's been very ill."

"What's wrong with him?" Douglas's heart sank. He had been banking heavily on a talk with his old chief.

"I don't know. But he can't teach. My *accoucheur* had to take one of his classes at the College, that's how I know. He was one of Dr Tait's students, like you."

"Like every doctor in Edinburgh worth his salt."

In a spacious dining room, next door to where they were to sleep, servants had already laid out a light supper. Douglas, used to visiting rich establishments, was not as impressed as his wife.

"Oh my, Clemmie! I'll never be the same again, after staying here! What a lovely, lovely house!"

"I'll take you all over it tomorrow," her hostess promised. "It impresses me too. It's so much more modern and convenient than the houses I grew up in, in France."

The bed was the widest and softest they had ever shared and Jean could scarcely bear to blow out the candles, she was so enthralled by the magnificence of the damask hangings and the upholstered headboard.

"Dougie, should we draw the curtains around us?'

"No. We need air. Settle down, Jeannie. I'm tired."

But neither one of them slept well. Her head was filled with the wonders of the house and how much money she could afford to spend smartening up her home-made dresses. Douglas was worrying about the possibility of meeting socially the judge who had given him the humiliating sentence, to say nothing of the less charitable among his old classmates. He was also concerned about Dr Tait.

Breakfast was lively, with the young Sincerbeaux vociferously objecting to doing lessons with their tutor while Angus and Tommy enjoyed themselves. It was a relief when Rabb showed up and offered to take the little Stewarts sightseeing.

"Go down to Cramond," Clementina suggested. "Let them run on the beach and paddle. Meg can stay here with the nursemaid. Will you be joining us for our midday dinner, Douglas?"

"No. I don't want to impose on you and I have several old friends I want to see."

"Well, just be back here by five o'clock because the concert is at six. It's in St Cecilia's Hall and we must be there in plenty of time to get good seats. Besides," she added," you will want to change, because we're going straight on to my uncle's party."

"Aye, you maun wear your evening suit," said Jean. "For I'll be a' dolled up, won't I, Clemmie?"

"Indeed yes! And here is the seamstress now, so let us go and look things out for her to work on."

"How do I find my way over to the Auld Toon?" Douglas asked.

"You just cross Charlotte Square and walk down to Princes Street and you'll see the Mound where it's always been."

II

Though Edinburgh had expanded enormously in ten years, it was easier than Douglas Stewart had expected to re-orient himself. The sun was shining. The air had the dry briskness he missed in the West, where showers from Loch Lomond kept the atmosphere damp. It was good to be out of the coach and walking again. Douglas had always preferred cities to country living, although, he now noticed, the inclines could be just as steep on pavements as on hilly paths and climbing the Mound was punishing to his weak leg. He'd need a horse or more likely a small trap if he moved back to the capital.

And did he really want to return to a place filled with such mixed memories?

Crossing the High Street, he glanced down towards the Tolbooth and shivered, remembering his brief incarceration there and its horrible climax.

Dr Tait's house on Nicolson Street looked just the same – solid, a little shabby and uncared for, since the old bachelor's interests lay elsewhere at the University and the Infirmary, both near by.

Douglas had to knock repeatedly on the door before it opened a chink and a small harried maidservant peeked out and announced, "The doctor's sick."

He smiled. "I'm not a patient. I'm an old student of his. Dr Stewart. I wrote . . ."

"Yes, and he received your letter," boomed a male voice as a big dark haired man appeared behind the maid and threw the door wide open. "Maggie, I'll take care of this gentlemen. Come in, sir. I'm Peter van Buren and happy to make your acquaintance." He held out a well-kept hand.

"Douglas Stewart. And I am also pleased to meet you, Mr . . . or is it Doctor . . . van Buren?"

"Doctor or what you will. Why not simply Peter since I hold the position you once had?" He looked a little old for a student and his accent was not Scottish.

Handing his hat to the maid, Douglas said, "I just arrived in town last night and heard Dr Tait had been taken ill. How is he?"

Peter van Buren took his arm and steered him into the well-remembered consulting room. After closing the door, he said, "There's no sense in alarming the household, but the Professor's in a bad way. He's had an apoplectic stroke."

"What's the prognosis?"

"Not good. You'll see for yourself."

"Maybe he shouldn't have visitors?"

"He'll want to see you. Your letter arrived yesterday and it aroused his first sign of interest. He's been totally apathetic, despairing, won't eat, won't try to exercise. Very difficult. And better let me go up and prepare him for your arrival. It would distress him if . . . for a second, he didn't recognise you." He tapped his forehead.

"Memory gone?"

"Some of it. Mostly for the present. He remembers the past all right. Sit down while I tell him you're here."

Douglas scarcely had time to look around the familiar room before Dr van Buren was back.

"He's pleased you've arrived. But be prepared for a big change in him."

Douglas nodded, bracing himself as they climbed the steep stair and entered a big, chilly uncurtained room. In a plain narrow bed lay an old man almost unrecognizable as the vigorous, ruddy-faced physician his student remembered so fondly.

"Dougie Stewart! Oh Dougie!" Watery blue eyes filled with tears as he struggled to hold out shaky hands. "Is it really yourself?"

"Aye, it's your bad penny turning up again, sir."

"Sit down, sit down, ye're as enormous as ever. Ye'll have met . . . met . . ." He waved vaguely towards Dr van Buren. "He's from America. . ."

Douglas pulled up a low chair and sat, bringing himself down as close as possible to the old man's level. "What's this about a stroke?"

"All down my left side. Peter, get him some whisky. Ye still like whisky, Dougie?"

"Yes, but it's too early in the day yet. And it's you I came to see. I need no refreshment."

Dr van Buren said, "I'll be downstairs making up prescriptions." And he quietly withdrew.

"A nice fellow," pronounced Dr Tait. "And clever. One of the best I've had since yourself."

"Has he been here long?"

"Aye. . . Aye. I canna recall exactly."

"And where does he hale from?"

"New York. New Amsterdam he calls it. The Dutch founded it and his family are patroons or whatever they ca' their landed gentry. He studied medicine in Philadelphia with old friends of mine from Edinburgh. He's been awful good to me since . . ."

"When did this happen, sir?"

"I'm . . . not sure. . . Dougie, what brings ye here? It's a real surprise."

"I wrote you a letter."

"Never got it. Never got it. Haven't heard from you in years."

Douglas knew well that he'd written regularly to his old mentor, and frequently since Primrose Paterson's death, for he had had to share his professional misgivings with someone. Now he knew why there had been no reply.

"I'm on my way to the Borders, sir. My mother is ill, terminally I fear, and she wants to see her grandchildren. I have my wife and family with me."

"Aye. . . aye. I mind you had children. I'd like to see them."

"Then I'll bring them here when we're on our way home. You'll be stronger then."

The old eyes filled again, "No. I'm finished, Dougie."

"You don't look finished to me. Your mind is clear and you have your powers of speech. What do your physicians say?"

"They'll tell me nothing. Nothing. Dougie, please. Look me over and give me the truth."

"Oh come now, Dr Tait. That would be presumptuous on my part."

"I'm requesting your professional opinion. I have a right to call you in on my case." He chuckled feebly. "I want to be sure you still know how to examine a patient, for a' yer fine bedside manner and . . ." his eyes roamed over his old student, "your two grey hairs."

"I came here on a social call, sir, without my bag. If you want me to give you my whole impressive performance, you'll have to supply me with a sand-glass and the rest of the paraphernalia."

"You need no sand-glass to estimate the damage. Hoist me up in bed and take a look."

With reluctant curiosity, Douglas eased him into a sitting position, testing reflexes as unobtrusively as he could. "Don't let me hurt you now, sir."

"Ye never hurt ony one if ye could help it. I mind that. Are you . . . are you still wastin your time wi that trance nonsense . . . that Mesmerism?"

"You mean animal magnetism and electricity?" So the old man wanted conversation. "As a matter of fact, I've developed my ability to use those forces. I can now, most of the time, put a patient to sleep whenever I want to, or at least erase their memories of pain. It's made me a popular surgeon in the West."

"Animal magnetism. Animal . . . manure. It's your voice, Dougie. You aye had such a soothin voice. And your air of authority. Patients believed you, whatever you telt them."

"Then I hope you too will believe me, when I tell you that you'd be better off sitting up than lying down and you must take some nourishment. With some work on your part, you could regain some of your mobility."

"Could I really, Dougie?"

Their eyes met. "You have to try, sir."

"But . . . it's hopeless, is it not? I'll never be the man I was."

"No. But hopelessness is an attitude you never permitted in your patients or your students either. There is always something that can be done you aye told us. Enough to make a difference to the way you will live from now on. Maybe you'll need help to walk or use your left arm, but as long as you have your mind and your voice you can still teach." He trusted that was true.

"You wouldna lie to me, would ye, Dougie?"

"I could never get away with that, sir." He stood up. "Now I'm going downstairs to tell . . . what's her name? Maggie? . . . to bring you up some broth and a wee glass of wine for your stomach's sake. And when I come back from the Borders, I want to find you sitting in that chair reading a book."

"When ye come back from the Borders, Dougie, I'll be dead."

"No!" He could not keep the urgency out of his voice. "Please be here, Dr Tait. I need you. Need to talk to you. . . About my future. . ."

"Your future?"

"What I should do with my life." But even as he said it, he knew Dr Tait was beyond advising anyone, though he clutched Douglas's hand and said, "Aye. Aye. I'll be thinking about ye and we'll talk when ye come back. And . . . bring your children to see me. *They're* your future, Dougie. What have ye for bairns?"

"Two wee boys and a girl."

The old man chuckled. "Ye rascal, ye'll have more yet."

"Maybe . . ." He disengaged himself gently. "Now I want your word that you'll take some nourishment. Will you?"

"Aye. Aye, Dougie."

"And I'll see you again after I've been to the Borders."

Clattering down the uncarpeted stair, trying to master his distress, he met the maid emerging from the cavernous kitchen.

"Maggie, do you have any soup made?"

"Aye, but he wouldna take it."

"He'll take it now. Heat it up quickly and give him a glass of wine, too."

Peter van Buren called from the consulting room, "Good for you, Stewart."

"Oh. I apologise. I didn't mean to prescribe without your permission."

"You don't need it. How about some whisky now?"

"I wouldn't say *no* to it."

"Then here you are, and I'll have some too." They toasted one another in silence.

"Sad, is it not? Such a great man," said van Buren.

Douglas nodded. "I'm on my way to visit his patients at the Infirmary," added the American. "Would you care to go with me? There are some interesting cases there at present."

Douglas's face lit up. "I can think of nothing I'd like better."

"Then maybe we can have something to eat at a pub. What do you fancy?"

"Some good fish fresh from Newhaven. Are there any oysters around?"

"We can find out."

"Then *Lead on, Macduff*. Sorry, I'm always quoting Shakespeare."

Peter van Buren smiled. He had, Douglas noticed enviously, a nearly complete set of teeth. "I whistle Mozart."

"My favourite modern composer. I'm going to hear some of his music later in the day."

"Oh. You'll be at that concert. So will I. My wife is a musician. She teaches piano. Dr Tait told me you used to be an amateur actor and a singer."

"I still sing."

They were as much at ease as if they had known each other all their lives.

III

"You mean to say you spent the whole day with sick people!" exclaimed Clementina when Douglas returned to Charlotte Square "Don't you get enough of them in Strathblane?"

"These people had different sicknesses. They were fascinating to me. I had a fine time, Clemmie."

"But you were supposed to use this day to rest and restore yourself before going on to Darnick."

"I did restore myself. I met a lot of old friends and made some new ones, including your *accoucheur*, who was over at the Infirmary. He's a very intelligent man."

"That means he agreed with everything Dougie telt him," remarked Jean.

"Aye. We discussed some cases." Particularly that of Primrose Paterson, although he had not named her. His eyes met his wife's. "I don't seem to be behind the times in obstetrics."

"But if you want to be in time for the concert, you had better start changing now."

"Willingly. I must be redolent of dirt and disease. But I did find my old barber who cut my hair and gave me a shave."

"Ye can have a bath, Dougie! They have hot water ready a' the time here. There's pipes up above the kitchen stove." Jean's eyes were shining. "It's the maist wonderfully convenient house I ever seen!"

"Some day you'll have one like it," he told her.

"Go to your bedroom, Douglas, and the servants will bring you the bath. I told Louis' valet to press your evening clothes so they're all ready. Jean's getting dressed upstairs, with me."

"Dougie, I'm wearing a new gown of Clemmie's that she canna get into. Wait till ye see me!"

"And we have to do her hair, too."

When they met again in the morning room, he scarcely recognised his wife. She wore a slim, straight, low-cut white dress of filmy cotton, the waist high under her handsome bosom, and over her shoulders she had draped a Paisley shawl. He had bought it for her when she was grieving for the stillborn child. White silk gloves covered her work-worn hands and her dark hair was piled high on top of her head, with artful curls over her forehead and ears. Around her neck hung a slim gold necklace with a little pendant, the only jewellery he had ever been able to afford. It matched a pair of earrings Walter Paterson had given her, years before, after she had nursed him back to health.

"Jeannie, you're beautiful!"

She smiled. "Ye look pretty handsome yersel, Dougie. I wish ye had more chances to wear that evening suit."

He turned to the Vicontesse. "Clemmie, will you please tell me honestly, is this coat still in style? I've had it for many years." It had been acquired during his one brief period of comparative affluence, as Dr Tait's assistant.

Clementina looked him over. "It's still reasonably fashionable. And that embroidered waistcoat is elegant."

"My wife made it."

"It's exquisite! Jean, you should take orders for these!"

"Oh, I do! I've made quite a bit of pin money that way. Clemmie, do I put the fan in ma wee bag?"

"Do you need a fan in a cold city like this?" asked Douglas.

"It may be hot in St Cecilia's Hall. They say five hundred people are coming to this concert and it's an old building without much ventilation. But surely you've been there before?"

"Aye, years ago and not that often. I'm more familiar with the old Theatre Royal on Shakespeare Square. I used to pick up pennies as an extra when the touring companies came to town. That's where I trained my voice."

"The actresses taught him," said his wife. "Or so he telt me."

"And none of them were as pretty as you are tonight."

"We were too busy with the seamstress to do any sightseeing," said the Vicomtesse, as they set off in the

Sincerbeaux' small town carriage. "And we won't see much of the city tonight because we're only going to the Cowgate and the view's all blocked off by a bridge. Most of the concerts are in the Assembly Rooms on George Street nowadays. When you come back from Darnick, Jean, you'll have to stay long enough to visit the Parliament House and Holyrood and all the historic places."

"And the boys want to see the Castle and the Royal Mile," said Douglas. He didn't plan to point out the Tolbooth.

The best seats in St Cecilia's Hall were rapidly filling up when they arrived. Peter van Buren, in smart evening clothes, was in the front row. He turned as the Vicomtesse's party entered and raised his hand in a nervous salute. He was by himself. He had mentioned that one of his children was ailing so possibly his wife had stayed home.

Looking over the audience, Douglas spotted another known figure, and nudged Jean. "See yon heavy fellow in the third row? Wi the fancy claret-coloured velvet jacket?" She nodded. "That's my enemy. The eminent Dr David Baxter. An important man at the Medical College these days, I hear. As if I didn't know. *Backsides* I used to call him."

"Shh, Dougie! The music's starting!"

The concert opened with the overture to *The Marriage of Figaro* which was enthusiastically received. Then the conductor left the stage, presumably to bring on the eminent virtuoso who was to play Mozart's 25th piano concerto.

But there followed such a long hiatus, the audience grew restless. Clementina whispered with Jean while her husband studied his programme and tried not to notice some curious glances in his direction.

Eventually, an official-looking individual appeared, to

announce that due, presumably, to some mishap of the stagecoach from London, the soloist had, regrettably, not yet arrived in Edinburgh.

The audience groaned.

"However," said the concert manager puffing out his chest, "we have been fortunate, at short notice, to secure the services of an American artiste now living in the city. She has performed this work in public many times, she tells me, in New York and throughout our colonies." He glanced quickly at a paper in his hand. "And her name is Mrs Peter van Buren."

"Johanna van Buren," corrected her husband's voice from the front row. "Ladies use their own names in *the old colonies*."

During the flurry of laughter, the conductor escorted onto the stage a tall young woman in a simple blue silk gown. Her straight dark hair was tucked under a white turban which highlighted a strong-featured handsome face.

As she settled herself at the piano, she acknowledged the applause with a brief nod. There was no music before her, but when the solo instrument took over after the long orchestral introduction, it was immediately apparent that she needed none. Her touch was masterly and her cadenza so individual and dramatic there was applause – quickly shushed – at the end of the first movement.

When she completed the final Allegretto, there was a standing ovation and she took many bows. The manager presented her with a bouquet of flowers and made a handsome speech, thanking her and hoping that she would perform with the orchestra again.

Johanna van Buren smiled as though well accustomed to praise and stepped off the stage to join her husband. She was immediately surrounded by well-wishers.

"Douglas, I must meet her!" exclaimed the

Vicomtesse. "And isn't he the American doctor you were telling us about?" Sweeping through the crowd with the Stewarts in tow, she approached the soloist, curtsied, and without waiting for an introduction, exclaimed, "Madame van Buren, I am overwhelmed with admiration!"

Peter's wife had dark eyes and an attractive smile. "Thank you, thank you. . ." Her eyes went questioningly to her husband, who in turn looked at Douglas.

"Johanna, let me present Dr Stewart, and, er . . . the Vicomtesse de Sincerbeaux, Mrs van Buren. And my wife, Jean. Madame, you are superb. I'm overwhelmed! Little did I realise, when your husband described you as a musician . . ."

"That she'd be performing tonight!" exclaimed Peter. "I didn't know myself, until I went home." He was bowing to Jean and Clementina. "Mrs Stewart . . . Madame de Sincerbeaux. . ."

"Doctor van Buren . . . Madame van Buren . . . I hope you can join us for a supper party after the concert. It's at my uncle's house. He's Lord Paterson and he lives on Heriot Row. I can take you in my carriage and will make sure you get safely home afterwards."

"Thank you. . . Thank you." The Dutchwoman had the same accent as her husband. "But . . . I'm afraid we cannot accept the invitation. My little daughter is sick. Another time, perhaps. . ." She looked up at Douglas. "My husband greatly enjoyed his visit with you, Dr Stewart."

"And I with him. But what is wrong with your child? Nothing serious, I trust?"

"No," said Dr van Buren. "Just a fine old Scottish cold. They've had them all year. It's the climate."

"Don't children catch colds in America?"

"Sure they do, but not as often. We have more sunshine."

"Well! Well!" cut in a loud male voice. "So the country doctor has come back to town! Remember me, Dougie?"

"I remember you, Backsides," said Douglas with ominous quietness, turning to face his old enemy.

"Haven't heard that nickname since you disappeared into the West. And what brings you to Edinburgh?"

"Personal matters."

"Ah. Dr Tait's probable retirement perhaps?"

"Dr Tait has no need to retire," said Douglas clearly. "He's making a good recovery. Is he not, Dr van Buren? . . . And do you know Dr Baxter?"

"We've met," said the American shortly.

"Well! Well! And what is happening to your practice, Dougie, while you enjoy the fleshpots here in town?"

"I left my partner in charge."

"Not that MacLean laddie, I trust? He'll kill off all your patients."

"Since he once saved my own life, I have no such fear."

"He's not overly blessed with brains."

Douglas took a deep breath. "He is caring and has plenty of common sense, qualities sometimes scarce among . . ." he paused, "fashionable physicians." He turned to his hostess. "Clementina, should we not be returning to our seats?"

Dr Baxter was eyeing Jean, who, in her borrowed finery, was one of the outstandingly handsome women in the concert hall.

"Aren't you going to introduce me to your wife, Dougie?"

What he wanted, more likely, was to be seen talking to the Vicomtesse de Sincerbeaux.

"I'll gladly introduce you to my wife when you introduce me to yours," said Douglas pleasantly. David

Baxter, notoriously, had never been interested in women.

Clementina turned, including the whole group in a vague, impersonal smile. "Yes, we'd better go back and find our seats, the intermission must be nearly over. Mrs van Buren, I am honoured to have heard you perform, and when the Stewarts come back from the Borders, I do hope you and your husband can come to supper and a musical evening at my house." She contrived to ignore Dr Baxter, although she did this with irreproachable politeness.

"Nicely done, Clemmie," Douglas murmured in her ear, as they sat down.

"I can't stand that man. He's so obnoxious, such a social climber. . . And not much of a physician either, I'm told. He owes his position at the College to the most blatant politics."

"D'you suppose. . ." Douglas started to say, but stopped, as the conductor mounted the podium. He had been about to ask her if it was possible Baxter seriously believed his own return to town was connected with Dr Tait's disabling sickness? If so, his old classmate must still consider him a threat, professionally. Interesting.

Clementina's uncle, Lord Paterson, lived in a large terrace house in the New Town, and as the Vicomtesse swept Jean and Douglas up the steps, another pair of guests arrived and greeted her.

"Well, Madame, and was your little Armand as seasick as he feared he'd be on his voyage to France?" asked the gentleman.

"Oh, no, Dr Gifford! Or at least if he was he didn't tell me." She took Douglas's arm. "And do you know . . ."

But the recognition on both sides was immediate and warm.

"Oh, you've met!"

"We have indeed We were classmates. Why didn't you let me know that you were coming to town?"

Douglas grinned. "Didn't know if you'd want to recognise me."

"For goodness sake! All that is past. We've a whole new climate in Edinburgh. Susan, this is my old friend, the legendary Dougie Stewart."

There was a round of introductions. Dr Gifford's wife was a pleasant young woman and did not intimidate Jean, whose social confidence increased when Lord and Lady Paterson welcomed her warmly. They had never met, for the circuit courts had not taken the jurist to the Blane Valley, but they were well aware of the close ties between the Stewarts and their nephew Walter.

In the high-ceilinged dining room, large platters of food were set out on a massive sideboard and liveried servants circulated among the guests, offering claret and wine.

A rapid, apprehensive glance around the company failed to offer Douglas any sign of the judge who had given him the humiliating sentence but he pulled Dr Gifford aside and asked, "What's become of Lord Braxfield?"

"Don't worry. He's dead."

"After a long and painful illness, I trust?"

"Probably. I don't know. But certainly complicated by too much drinking. A horrible man and everyone admits it now. The witch-hunts are over, Dougie, we're all liberals these days. Even so," he added, "we still have more lawyers than doctors, and all the successful ones are here tonight."

The chief topic of conversation was the concert and Johanna van Buren's performance. "Who is she?" an elegant lady with a plumed headdress asked Clementina. "We saw you talking to her as if you were well acquainted."

"Dr Stewart knows her husband. Douglas, this is Lady

Weir. Tell her about the van Burens." Clementina swept another young woman into the group. "*Charlotte! Ici c'est Dr Stewart qui connais bien Docteur van Buren, et ce monsieur me dit que le Marquis de Lafayette est encore bien connu en Amérique, un grand hero de leur Revolution.*"

"*Ah, oui! Les Lafayettes.*" While the two young women chattered in French, Douglas told Lady Weir what little he knew of the American couple.

Lord Paterson joined them to extricate escape from the gossipy old lady. "Dr Stewart, I'm afraid you'll miss seeing Walter's mother in Strathblane. She just went there with my daughter Betsy. They hope to console him a bit. So tragic about Primrose."

Douglas nodded. "But at least there is now an heir."

"True. And he will carry on the Paterson name, for all I sired were girls. You come originally from the Borders, I understand? You must meet . . ." He beckoned to a tall man at the centre of a lively group around the fireplace. "He's editing a collection of ballads . . . Wattie! Come over here and meet a fellow Borderer. Didn't Clemmie say you were en route to Melrose, Dr Stewart?"

"We are actually going to Darnick, which is close by. My father is the parish minister there."

"An interesting little town," said the tall man, as he joined them. He had a pronounced limp, though he walked confidently and it did not detract from his handsomeness. Holding out his hand, he smiled and remarked, "Does the Stewart clan have an offshoot in the Borders?"

"My full name is Douglas Elliot Stewart."

"Ah! 'My name is Little Jock Elliot, and wha' daur meddle wi me?'"

"Precisely. Where do you hale from, sir?"

"Well, I was born in Edinburgh but I spent my childhood convalescing from an illness among the Eildon

Hills. The loveliest country in the world."

"I agree," said Douglas. "I prefer it to the West, where I am now in practice. Although . . . have you ever seen the Blane Valley?"

"That was Rob Roy's territory, was it not?"

"Yes, indeed. There's a big tree in Blanefield said to be his trysting place with the local farmers. They bribed him to let their cattle alone."

"I must see that when next I visit Loch Lomond. It's good riding country."

"Excellent. I make most of my calls on horseback."

"You're a doctor?"

"Yes, and speaking as a medical man, forgive my curiosity but I notice you've had some trouble with your leg. I also am lame and, since we must be about the same age and both grew up in the Borders, I'm wondering if our problem comes from the same source? I've often thought there must have been other cases. Did you have a high fever and terrible pain which left you with paralysed muscles?"

"I did indeed. Fortunately I was too young to remember much about the pain, but I do remember vividly being rolled in the coat of a newly slaughtered sheep in hope of improving my leg's performance."

Douglas shook his head. "What they used to do in the name of medical science! Do you know of any others who suffered as we did?"

The big man shook his head. He had an attractive smile and brilliant blue eyes. "No. But I was never curious. As you are, from a professional standpoint. I have never allowed my crooked leg to stop me doing whatever I wanted. Obviously the same is true of yourself. You don't even limp."

"I have a special boot made to my specifications. It

corrects my balance. But my handicap has never held me back. Indeed, I credit it with inspiring me to become a doctor."

"And for me, I suppose, my infirmity made me a reader . . . and now a writer."

"D'you suppose our Border stubbornness helped us to overcome?"

"Most likely," agreed the tall man.

"Now tell me, please about your ballad collection. As an amateur singer, I'm very fond of ballads."

On their way back to Charlotte Square, Douglas asked Clementina, "Who was that fellow I had such a good talk with?"

"You had good talks with a lot of people! You were quite a social lion. Which man do you mean?"

"An advocate. He was lame and even taller than me. I didn't catch his name, but his wife was French and he's just edited a collection of poetry called *The Minstrelsy of the Scottish Borders.* I'd like to buy a copy for my mother."

"Oh, you mean Charlotte's husband. I don't think the book's published as yet. At least, she was complaining to me that he was still getting up at five every morning and scribbling away for hours before he went to the Parliament House. But his name is easy to remember. It's Scott. Walter Scott."

IV

It said a lot for the Vicomtesse's ability to manage her household staff that the Stewart family were able to make a good start for the Borders next morning. While Douglas and Jean were having breakfast, the little Sincerbeaux's nurse dressed and fed the children. The valet and

Clementina's maid packed the luggage and loaded it into the big carriage, under Rabb Innes's supervision. The cook filled a hamper with food and drink.

The actual departure, however, was hectic, the children were so excited. As soon as they left Charlotte Square behind, passed the Meadows and were heading out towards open country, Angus peered out of the carriage window and wanted to know, "Are these the Eildon Hills, Papa?"

"No. They're the Braids. And then we pass the Pentlands."

"Are we going to Cramond?" asked Tommy.

"No. That's in the other direction. What did you see down there, yesterday? You were both sound asleep when I came back to change for the concert. You must have been tired out."

"Aye, they were that," said Jean.

"We seen the sea," announced Angus.

"I paddled in it," said Tommy.

"And Rabb took us to a pub and we had steak and kidney pudding . . . Mama, I want a hard boiled egg. I seen them being packed."

"No. Ye canna possibly be hungry after a' that porridge."

"And we've a long way to go so we're not picnicking until we're at the top of Soutra Brae," said his father.

"That's a fair distance, Doctor," Rabb called down from his seat on the box. "Do you boys want to come up here wi me, the way ye did yesterday and gie your parents a chance to catch their breath?"

"Aye, please!"

"Don't let them make a nuisance of themselves, Rabb," Douglas said.

"Naw, naw, sir! I enjoy their company."

Little Meg remained inside with her parents, cuddling a doll Clementina had given her.

"What's your baby's name?" her father asked.

She looked blank.

"Ye know her name," Jean prompted. "Ss. . . Ssoo. . ."

"Susie," said the little girl with a sweet, triumphant smile.

"Ye see, Dougie? She does understand . . . do ye not, ma wee doo? She can talk when she wants to."

The child's backwardness had bothered him for some time, but there was no doubt about her physical perfection. She had soft golden curls, a flawless skin, and her mother's dark eyes. If she grew up to be as beautiful as she was now, but did not develop mentally, he wondered what would become of her.

But for the moment at least she was no problem. She fell asleep on Jean's lap and never wakened when he carefully moved her, to be closer to his wife.

"How did ye like Edinburgh, ma dear?"

She sighed. "It was wonderful. And that house . . ."

When he wearied of her enlarging on its modern wonders, he asked, "And what did ye think of the company we met?"

"Oh. Clemmie's friends were awful nice to me. But I liked Mrs van Buren the best for I was the most at ease wi her. I didna have to worry about ma accent. Did ye like her husband?"

"Aye, he's an excellent doctor, at least from what I saw. He trained in Philadelphia, tells me there's a growing medical college there."

"Oh, Dougie! Ye're no thinkin' of going to America surely? No after the welcome ye got in Edinburgh."

"How about Davie Baxter? I wonder if the town's big

enough yet to hold both of us. And besides . . . I don't know. You can't put back the clock, can you?"

"Ye'll find out when we get to Darnick," she told him. "Dougie, I was up gey early and I'm weary. Will ye keep an eye on Meg while I hae a wee nap?"

Was she breeding again? he wondered in passing. But usually the morning sickness was her first symptom.

Putting a protective arm around his daughter, he tried to sleep but there was too much on his mind. And, though he was not a man who valued scenic beauty, he could not stop himself from looking out of the window to enjoy the countryside, one of the better memories of his youth.

The fields of yellow corn had a lush warmth lacking in the West. The distant hills were rounded and less rugged and there was plenty of greenery in the deep ravines and along the banks of the turbulent rivers. More trees than in the Blane Valley marked the boundaries of rich estates, whose owners lived in large stone residences, grey with age.

The ancient Border towns, small and also grey, showed signs of recent prosperity, he observed, and a huge agricultural fair was going on in one of them, which slowed down their progress.

"How do they mak' their living here?" Jean asked, wakening up and also looking out of the window.

"They farm. And weave the wool from all those sheep."

The view tilted as they bumped over the old drover road. Then suddenly the heavy vehicle came to a stop and Rabb called out, "We're on the Soutra Aisle!"

Angus and Tommy tumbled down from the coachman's seat and started chasing each other. As Douglas helped his wife out of the carriage, she shivered and pulled her shawl around her. "Eh! That wind's cold!"

"Aye. Straight off the Firth of Forth." He inflated his lungs, suddenly happy. "Look, boys! Ye can see the sea away in the distance – and yon's the Fife coast behind it."

But the children were more interested in the contents of the hamper. It held mutton and game pies, cold sliced fowl and a big slab of cooked salmon. For dessert there were apples, oranges and a couple of lemons, to say nothing of a poke of hard candy. To wash everything down, the children had lemonade, while the grownups sipped ale and chilled wine.

They picnicked seated on an old plaid Rabb unearthed in the storage area in the coach.

"Can we see the Eildon Hills now, Papa?" Angus asked.

"Why are you so anxious to see the Eildons?"

"Because ye telt me that was where King Arthur was buried wi a' his Knights o' the Round Table. And . . . and Thomas the Rhymer . . . and . . . and a' the battles like Otterburn."

Douglas burst into song:

March! March! Ettrick and Teviotdale!
Why the de'il dinna ye march forward in
              order?
March! March! Eskdale and Liddesdale,
All the Blue Bonnets are bound for the Border!

"Ye maun learn that one to sing to yer Granny. She taught it to me when I was your age." He hoisted them to their feet and they paraded up and down, picking up the tune and the words, all three capering on the roadside grass.

"Ye're actin' like a laddie yersel!" Jean remarked.

"Aye, it's good to be back in the Borders."

"When do we get to Darnick?" asked Tommy.

"In a wee while. We go through Melrose first."

"Aye, and from that point, doctor, ye'll hae to guide

me," said the coachman. "For the stable hands in Edinburgh only gie'd me directions for the main roads."

"I'll guid ye. We're still a long way off. And Rabb, if you think the horses are tiring, we could stop over for the night at Stow or Galashiels."

"Naw, naw, sir. The beasts have been o'er rested this past month. And these highways are far better than I'd expected. They're laying guid roads in the Borders. Forby, the days are long the now, if ye dinna mind arrivin a wee bittie late."

So they packed up the remains of the picnic and rumbled on, the boys once again inside the coach. They would not keep still. They tumbled over each other and their mother and little sister at every lurch. Several times their father had to break up fights.

The whole family was nervous and tired by the time the ruins of Melrose Abbey appeared in the distance and Rabb pulled up.

The boys jumped down and would have started racing around again but Jean called them back. "Naw! We maun change yer clothes! Ye're to look yer best when ye arrive! Dougie, leave Meg in the coach she's a' tidy, but get out of the way. Ye dinna need a clean shirt, do ye?"

"No. I put one on this morning, but I'd like to freshen myself."

"There's a wee bit stream down there to the left, Doctor," said Rabb. "I'll be drawing water for the horses from it when ye've finished."

There were bushes too. Douglas went behind them, thankful to be alone. For suddenly it came over him that he was nearly home – or at least close to his father's house.

His father.

If I was a believer, Douglas thought, I'd be praying.

Instead, he emptied his bladder and rinsed his hands

in the icy burn, wishing they had lingered at the country fair as the children had wanted to do, or decided to stop overnight in Galashiels. It was too late to change plans now.

"Jean, gie me ma hat and coat. It's turning chilly. Are ye finished dressing the boys?"

"Aye. . ."

He swung himself up onto the coachman's box and pointed out to Rabb a narrow track veering off from the outskirts of Melrose. "You see yon old building down on the left? Yon's a peel tower. It's belonged to the Heiton family since the fourteenth century. And it's close to Darnick village. That's the way you go. And Rabb. . ."

"Aye, sir?"

"After you've taken us to the Manse and unloaded the luggage, go to the Inn. You should find it around the corner from the kirk. Have yourself a good meal with plenty o' drinks for you've earned them and take a room. Here's some money on account." He drew a handful of coins from his pocket. "And, er. . ."

"Aye?"

"Buy me a wee flask of whisky and slip it to me when no-one's looking. My father never allowed me a dram." Douglas had once treated Rabb for a serious injury. He had also, on occasions, suggested remedies for ailments of the Leddrie Green horses. They were old friends.

"Ye'd be no but a laddie when last ye were here, sir?"

"Aye. And I'm a grown man now and things may be different. But you never can tell. . ."

They bumped down the hill, followed the dirt road past Darnick Tower and into the village. "Is yon yer faither's kirk?" Rabb took a hand off the reins and pointed to a small grey building surrounded by a graveyard.

"Aye. And just beyond it is the Manse. Behind those

trees. There's the gate. Let me down."

Rabb's indistinct command to the horses stopped them in their tracks.

V

"We're here," Douglas called down to his family. "I'm going ahead to announce our arrival."

His stomach churning, he jumped down, smoothed his stock, made sure his topcoat was buttoned, and settled his beaver hat firmly over his windswept hair. Squaring his shoulders, he strode up the familiar path, taking care not to limp.

The flower beds, which he remembered as well trimmed, were now overgrown and choked with weeds. The Manse itself looked smaller and less overpowering than in the past. The woodwork around the windows needed painting. Maybe he noticed these things because he was now a householder himself.

Taking a deep breath, he tirled at the unpolished pin on the front door. And when a slatternly servant opened it, he tipped his hat as he did when making a professional call, bowed politely and announced in a carrying voice, "I am Doctor Stewart from Strathblane. I am expected."

She gulped, put her hand to her mouth and stood aside to let him into the dark, cold hall.

Then a door flew open and a tiny figure staggered out.

"Dougie! It's my Dougie! Oh Dougie! Oh . . . oh . . . at last. . ."

"Mama!" He caught her in his arms. She had never been a stout woman but now she was so thin he would never have recognised her. Until he saw her huge, dark eyes as loving as ever in her emaciated face.

"Oh, Dougie! Dougie!"

They were both crying. As he held her close, he felt the terrible deterioration in her flesh and knew they had arrived none too soon.

"We . . . we were expecting you yesterday . . . and the day before . . . every day since we got your letter!" She was toothless but the smile she beamed on him was beautiful. "Oh, Dougie! You're bigger than ever! And just the same! But, but . . ." her little hands moved over his face, wiping off the tears, "you've grey hairs!"

"I'm an old man now, Mama."

"You're thirty four!"

"I thought I was thirty-three, but you should know." They were laughing, holding each other at arm's length.

"And . . . you're handsome! I knew you'd grow up to be handsome!"

"Don't be daft, Ma. I'm just the same big lout. And you. . ." He couldn't tell her she was unchanged.

"Come away in!" She took a step forward, staggered, nearly fell. He caught and held her.

"You shouldn't be standing in the cold."

"Dougie! Let me go! For . . . look! Look! Are these my grandchildren?"

Jean had followed him up the path, the little girl in her arms and the boys, holding hands, just ahead.

The old lady, tears flowing, stretched out both hands in welcome.

"This is Angus Elliot, Mama. And Thomas Mac-Dougal." The two boys, as they had been instructed, bowed low. "And Margaret, who's named after you. We call her Meg. And their mother . . . Jean."

"Your bonnie, bonnie wife. Oh, my dear!"

Jean curtsied then impulsively reached out and kissed

her mother-in-law. Somehow, he got them all into the house, giving Rabb a quick signal to stay where he was.

"Dougie!" said another female voice, and turning, he found his sister, Jennifer, who had been in her teens when he had last seen her. She was tall and thin, with mousy hair scraped up under a cap, but she had a sweet face.

"Jenny!" He kissed her. She smelt of baking. "My wife Jean. . ." The two women curtsied, hesitated, then hugged each other.

Mrs Stewart grabbed a walking stick from the hall stand and moved herself and the boys into a small room where, he remembered, the family had always gathered.

Jenny said to her brother, "You must have baggage. And before he went out, Father told me where you were all to sleep." So the old man wasn't around. Douglas called to Rabb to bring in their trunk and valises.

"Upstairs," Jenny directed, and led the way. "Father said you're to be in your old room, Dougie, with the two boys. Your wife and the wee girl are to have the spare bed."

He grinned at her. "Not so fast! The boys can go here." He ushered Rabb into a tiny dark chamber with three trundle beds. "But if he thinks I can fit into yon wee couch, he's mistaken." He strode across the hall, threw open another door. "Aye. This is more like it. A good big bed I can share with Jean."

"But, Dougie, Father said . . . "

"He can say what he likes. I sleep with my lawfully wedded wife." How else, he wondered, would he ever get through the visit? Jenny looked scared.

"Dinna fash yersel," he said, remembering how the minister hated his using the vernacular, "Why should he ken? . . . And now he's rid o' the bags, let me introduce you to Rabb Innes, who drove us here. He'll stay at the inn . . . which I presume is still there?"

She nodded. The spare bedroom faced the road, and as she glanced out of the window her eyes widened.

"My! What a fancy carriage! You must be doing well for yourself, Dougie."

"He should, for he's a guid doctor," said Rabb, unburdening himself of the last hand valise. "There's a big hamper wi food, miss. Should I put it in the kitchen?"

"Yes. Please. It's . . . in the back, downstairs."

"I'll find it," said the coachman. He looked at Douglas. "D'ye want to see me later this evening, sir?" A discreet way of asking when the doctor needed his whisky.

"No thanks, Rabb. You have had a long day. But come by the morn, if you please. We may want you to drive us somewhere."

Touching his forelock, Rabb Innes left, leaving the brother and sister alone on the landing.

"How is she, Jenny?"

"Dr Matheson says she's dying."

"Matheson. Is he good with her?"

"Yes. He's a nice man." Her pale cheeks turned a faint pink. "But . . . Father won't let her take the medicines he prescribed for the pain."

"Why not?"

"He says she'd become a slave to them, an opium eater . . . and she suffers terribly, Dougie."

"I'll give her something. I'll take care of him, too, if need be."

"Oh Dougie, don't start a fight! It would kill her!"

"Don't worry, wee sister. I'm a doctor now, and I know how to handle these situations."

"I hope you do. He's been so difficult, I don't know how much longer I can stand it here. Only for Mama's sake. . . We'd better go down now or she'll wonder what we're talking about. . . "

He wanted to know more about the drugs his father had prohibited, but the two boys were clattering up the uncarpeted stair, eager to see their room.

Jenny hustled them cheerfully along the landing. "I've found all your papa's old toys. There's a rocking horse and wee wooden animals. And books."

"Not those dreadful tomes about tortured Christian martyrs!" exclaimed Douglas.

She laughed. "No. They're in the study nowadays."

In the morning room, Jean, already at ease with her mother-in-law, had taken off her bonnet and Meg's. The old lady lay on the sofa with a rug over her and when her son came in, her thin face lit up with happiness.

"Whaur's ma grandfather?" demanded Angus, rushing back downstairs with Tommy in tow.

"He's out visiting people in the village," Mrs Stewart told him. "But he'll be back for his supper. Maybe when he sees the coach . . . Darnick's such a wee place you can hardly miss it . . . he'll come home sooner." God forbid, thought Douglas, his stomach contracting.

"Are you hungry?" Jenny asked. "I've bannocks all made . . . is that still your favourite, Dougie? . . . and there's tea and ale and, and whatever you want. . . "

"No thank ye, we had a picnic," Jean began to say when Tommy announced, "I'm hungry the now."

"Then come with Auntie Jenny and we'll see what we can find to eat."

"But not too much to spoil his appetite," Jean cautioned.

"Tell me a' about Edinburgh, son." Mrs Stewart stretched out her hand and Douglas sat down beside her. "I hear you stayed in a beautiful house in the New Town."

"Aye. Jean will never feel the same again about our wee butt and ben in Strathblane."

"We have a bonnie hoose," said Jean loyally. "It's small but it's comfortable."

"Are your parents living, dear?"

"No. But we named Angus after ma faither. He was still alive when Dougie and I met."

"And he didn't like me, Ma."

"He didna want ye taking me away from the farm. I . . ." Jean had to make that confession, "I did much o' the work. We were puir."

"But when she came to the kirk, she was aye so smartly dressed, I thought she must be an heiress."

"So that was the attraction. I thought it was ma cooking . . . a' those drop scones ye ate whenever ye came on a professional visit."

"Aye, she always fed me well, Mama. I liked making calls at that farm. Jean's auntie was the midwife when I came to Strathblane and I learned a lot from her. Not just about childbirth, but herbs and potions." Which might introduce the subject of painkillers.

But at that moment, the heavy front door slammed, and once again Douglas tensed. A booming benevolent male voice inquired, "And who might *you* be, little man?"

A clear childish treble answered, "I'm Angus Elliot Stewart and you maun be my grandfather."

Douglas caught his mother's eye. "I suspect," she remarked, "that your father has finally met his match."

The minister made his entrance. Tall like his son, he was an impressive figure in clerical black, with thick white hair tied back in an old-fashioned queue. He had handsome features and gleaming dark eyes, and there was a strong family resemblance between him and his elder grandson, now holding his hand and beaming ecstatically at him. Douglas stood up, tongue tied.

"Well! Well!" said the Reverend Mr Stewart. "So you

have all arrived safely." He approached Jean who rose quickly and curtsied. "My dear, welcome to Darnick. I am glad you have come with your husband."

He acknowledged his son's presence with a nod. At least the first meeting was over. Now Tommy ran in.

"And who are you, young man?" asked the minister.

"Thomas MacDougal Stewart, and I was ca'ed after you."

"Sir," prompted Douglas.

"Sir."

"Since you are my namesake, surely you should address me as Grandfather."

"Granfaither," repeated the little boy in his flat West of Scotland accent.

The maid and Jenny were bringing in trays of food. The table had been set and by the time they were seated, with Meg in a little highchair Douglas well remembered, the first awkwardness had passed.

"I trust you had a comfortable journey, son," said Mr Stewart. "Does that handsome carriage outside the Inn belong to you?"

"No. One of my patients in Strathblane gave me the use of it." Douglas turned to his mother. "His sister put us up in Edinburgh."

"The *Vicomtesse de Sincerbeaux*," said Jean in her best accent. "She's married to a French nobleman."

"And they live on Charlotte Square, Thomas," added Mrs Stewart.

"Indeed. Then I trust your quarters here won't be too humble for you." The minister unfolded a large white linen table napkin and looked across the table challengingly. "Pronounce the blessing, if you please, son."

Douglas stood up, motioning to Angus and Tommy to do the same. Lowering his eyes, he recited tonelessly:

Some hae meat that canna eat
And some hae nane that want it.
But we hae meat and we can eat
And so the Lord be thankit.

He sat down, thankful that his children, unused to grace before supper, had not started demanding and consuming food as promptly as they did at home.

"Why, Dougie! That's the Selkirk Grace," exclaimed Mrs Stewart. "You remembered it!"

"It seemed appropriate in the Borders."

When the ashettes had been handed around and everyone had a full plate, Douglas asked, addressing the company at large, "Where are my brothers and what are they doing?"

"Kenneth has a sheep farm," said Mrs Stewart. "He sells his wool to mills in Galashiels. Cloth is a big industry here nowadays."

"Aye, and in the Blane Valley, too," put in Jean. "I'm awful interested in spinning and weaving. My cousin owns an inkle factory in Strathblane. Do you think I might visit some of the manufacturers? I'd like to see what they have."

"Yes, of course, my dear," said the minister affably. "You can go to Galashiels and to Hawick and Duns too, since you have a carriage at your disposal. Kenneth will advise you on what to see. He might even accompany you."

So Father's strategy is to charm my wife and children, thought Douglas. The old man can do it too, when so inclined.

"Is Kenneth married?" Again he addressed them as a group.

"Yes, and he has a wee girl," responded Mr Stewart. "You'll be seeing them for they know of your coming. Although of course you sent us no details as to when you would arrive."

"That was hard to do since we were dependent on circumstances we could not completely control," replied Douglas equably. "And the coachman had no knowledge of the state of the roads."

"Kenneth and Effie should be here tomorrow," said Jenny. "They usually come to see Mama on a Friday."

"And Alasdair?"

"Your younger brother is studying divinity in Edinburgh. Had you given us more information about your plans, I could have sent you his address and you might have seen him."

"I can do so on my return to town, sir. How long has he been at the college?"

"This is his second year and he is making his mark as a brilliant student."

Douglas restrained himself from commenting that his brother must have changed, having been notoriously thickheaded in school. He turned towards his sister. "And what about you, Jenny? How have you escaped matrimony?"

"Jennifer is young yet," said her father." And not yet ready to leave home."

She must be at least twenty-four, almost a spinster. Had her suitors been scared away?

"You're not eating, Dougie," said his mother, as the meal progressed.

"I'm not hungry. We had a picnic at the top of Soutra and the air was so bracing I ate more than I should."

"And you didn't need to bring us salmon," said Jenny. "We've plenty in the Tweed. Trout too. But that fruit is a real treat. Mama, have an orange. I'll cut it up for you."

"Let me," said her son. He slit the skin with surgical neatness and separated the segments. It gave him something to do.

But the old lady ate only one piece and divided the rest between Tommy and Angus. She was beginning to move restlessly in her chair. "Jean . . . my dear, I'm weak from all the excitement. . . I must go to my bed, so excuse me. I'm fair happy you're here and the wee ones too. . . Dougie, take me upstairs, if ye please."

"Yes, of course, Mama." He started to rise.

"Sit still, son," ordered the minister. "I will carry your mother up later when we have completed our repast."

"Oh, please, Thomas! I want to go the now." Mrs Stewart's voice rose sharply. "I'm weary. And I want Dougie to take me. He's younger than you, and big and strong. . ." Under the table she sought out her son's hand and squeezed it hard.

"But he has not finished his supper." Mr Stewart looked annoyed.

"I have enough, thank you, sir. "Every inch a physician, Douglas met his father's eyes for the first time. "My mother must be exhausted. Say goodnight to your granny, boys. You'll see her the morn. Jenny, hold this door open for me, please."

He stood up and gathered the old lady in his arms, carried her out and up the staircase. From the way her fingers dug into him he knew she was in pain.

"Are you in the same room, Mama?"

"No. I've been in ma wee sewing place, since I've been so sick."

Next door to the master bedroom was a pretty little antechamber which had always been her private domain. Now it held a bed, already turned down and warmed with hot bricks.

Jenny was behind them, with candles and a tray holding a tumbler and a pitcher of milk. "Dougie, I'll undress her."

But his mother was clinging urgently to his hand. "Don't go away, son. I must speak with you."

"I'll come back, Mama. Do you have medicine to take?"

Jenny shook her head.

"Then I'll prepare some for you." He went quickly to the spare room and found his bag, glad that he had stocked it well with opiates.

To give his sister time, he made a quiet reconnaissance of the Manse's upper floor. Dusk was falling but there was still enough light to see the layout. He had already seen the room he had once shared with his two brothers, and which his sons would now occupy. Jenny, as in the past, slept next door. The big front bedroom, once filled with his mother's presence, was now starkly masculine and looked as if it had been so for some time.

"You can come back in, Dougie," his sister called. She had settled Mrs Stewart in bed, well wrapped in a shawl. The two candles gave good light, for it was still early evening and the tall windows were uncovered. "Do you aye carry that bag? Even when ye're away on holiday?"

He nodded. "Habit, I suppose. And Jean was worried the bairns might fall sick. They've never been so far beyond Strathblane before."

"They were blooming when they arrived here!"

"Aye, they were much too interested in seeing the sights to even think of vomiting in the carriage, as I'd feared." He found a chair and moved it up beside the bed.

"Shall I look in and see you later, Mama?" Jenny asked.

"Aye, but no until I've talked with Dougie."

Her daughter left, closing the door.

"Turn the key, son," the old lady ordered.

"Do we need to do that?"

"Aye. We do."

Her voice was so feverishly urgent he did as she asked. Then, sitting down again, he took both her hands in his, unobtrusively searching for her pulse. "Where do you have pain, Mama?"

She sighed. "Everywhere, it seems, and most of the time now. And . . . bad."

"What do you take for it?"

"Nothing. Your father says I must go to meet my Maker with a clear mind. *No more of this drugging,* he telt Dr Matheson."

He was so angry it must have shown, for she went on defensively, "He means the best for my soul's sake, Dougie."

"Your soul needs no help in the Hereafter, Mama. But your body does, while you're still on earth." He let her go, reached down into his bag. "I'm putting some drops in your milk and you're to drink all of it at once. Now."

She pushed the tumbler away.

"No. Later, maybe, but not now."

"Why not? If you're worrying about Father, you can tell him I gave you a herbal drink, made from flowers." Poppies, after all, were the basic ingredient in laudanum.

From the little smile she gave, he knew she understood. "Dougie, I'll drink it in due course. But now I must talk to you."

"Could we not do that in the morning, when you're rested?"

"No! No! I'm that far gone, I could sleep away, and . . . there's something." She gestured towards a chest of drawers where she had always stored linens. "Look in the secret compartment, son, you'll mind that from when you were a wee boy. You were aye playing with it, hiding things."

He remembered it well.

"Open it," she ordered. "Now."

Recognizing the urgency in her voice, he fingered the wood. Something connected and a slot shot out.

"There's a key in there, is there not, son?"

"Aye. There is."

"It opens the bottom drawer."

He inserted it, pulled, and drew out the long heavy compartment.

She was sitting up in bed, her eyes gleaming. "What d'y'see there, laddie?"

He stared. "Money. Rolls and rolls of bank notes. Gold. . ."

"It's yours, Dougie. Your inheritance as an Elliot. From me."

His eyes met hers in disbelief. "What do you mean?"

She slid down in bed, panting. "When he disowned you, I started selling my jewellery, piece by piece. It was mine from my dowry. And I began tithing. Every penny he gave me to buy things for the household, I saved a part. I made jam and cakes and sold them to families in the village. And I wove cloth, sold it to the gentry in the big houses. He never knew. Whenever I had enough, I took the coins to the Inn and turned them in for bills."

Douglas stared. "All those years. . . Didn't he suspect?"

"He never goes to the Inn. They would never tell him either."

"But . . . Mama! He's your husband. It's his money."

"No! No, it isn't! I was a rich woman when he married me. I had a good tocher and he got it all. It's what furnished this Manse and bought all those books of his. I didn't mind when it was paying for your education but then he turned you out, and for no reason except that you wouldn't do his bidding. And never asked me, never even let me kiss you and bless you and wish you God Speed. You were my son too. It was not right, what he did. . . Women should have rights, Dougie. Should they not?"

"A lot of them have been saying so, since we've had all these arguments about the Rights of Man."

"Aye, and there was a woman that wrote a book. Mary Woll . . . Woll . . ."

"Mary Wollstonecraft?"

"Aye. I never read it but I heard about it. The Vindication of the Rights of Women. That was the name of it." Her eyes closed and she looked so spent, he moved quickly to the bedside. But she was not gone, although she looked close to it. "Dougie. Take a pillowslip from the drawer above and put the money in it. Now. And put it to your room. Hide it in your trunk."

"Mama . . . I can't do that. . . I . . ."

She opened her eyes and looked at him challengingly. "Are you so feared of him yet you'd go against my dying wish?"

"No, I'm not feared of him, but . . . Mama . . ."

"Wheesht. Nobody knows it's there, not even Jenny. It's yours. I saved it for you."

"Oh no . . . Mama. I canna. . ."

"Oh, Dougie, I've been desperate to get it into your hands! I've stayed alive to do it and I'm that frail. . ."

He didn't know what to think. He needed Jean.

"Mama, let me go get ma wife."

She sat up again, "No! Later on, you can tell her. But now it's between you and me." Weak tears were pouring down her thin cheeks.

"Oh, please, Dougie . . . I've lived on in agony just for this . . . to see it in your hands. . ."

And she made no attempt to hide the spasm of pain.

He caught her, held her, his fingers probing. "Where is it worst, Mama? I'm a doctor, mind! Maybe I can help you. . ."

"In my breasts and my back. . ."

He could feel the tumours through her nightgown, and was shocked. "Mama, please drink that milk."

She pulled away from him. "I'll not drink anything until you've taken your inheritance. I mean it, Douglas Elliot."

He remembered that note in her voice from his boyhood. And when she used his full name, he had always obeyed her because he knew he must. "Where did you say that . . . pillowcase?" She pointed at a drawer. It was unlocked and filled with household linens. Carefully, he transferred the rolls of bills. He had never seen so much money in his life.

"Take it into your own room," she ordered. "But make sure first that there's nobody about."

He unlocked the door. Sounds of bedtime scrimmaging came from the boys' room and Jean's voice raised in admonition. The hall was dark and no light shone from under the door of the master bedroom.

As if reading his mind, Mrs Stewart whispered, "Your father will be in his study. He aye reads the Scripture afore he comes to bed. Jenny and the lassie will be cleaning up in the kitchen. It's now or . . . or maybe never, Dougie."

He picked up the pillowslip, carried it to the spare bedroom where he pushed it under the bed, well out of sight. Then he came back and gathered up the coins. There was just enough space for them in his bag among the bottles and the instrument case.

"Mama, ye're making make me feel like a thief in the night." Rotten, he could hear his father saying, rotten to the core.

"No! You're the heir to the Elliots. My first-born. My favourite child. . ." Her eyes filled. "Give me that medicine now, son." He held the tumbler to her lips. "Now talk to me," she said. "Tell me all about your life. . ."

"What sort of things?"

"Everything since you left. . . Are you happy?"

"I suppose so. In my marriage, aye, but in my work. . ."

"Are you not content with it?"

He shook his head. "I've still far to go for that."

She squeezed his hand. "Maybe. . . now . . ."

Maybe now he could move on. Trying, as he so often did in his practice, to use his voice to soothe, he started talking – about Strathblane, his children, his cases, the visit to Edinburgh – holding her in his arms, trying to lessen her suffering with the touch of his fingers.

She was starting to respond when, after a single knock, the door opened.

"I trust I may come in and bid goodnight to my wife," said the Reverend Mr Stewart.

Douglas stood up, his heart pounding. He had no thought for himself. He was afraid for his mother. Jenny had been right – the slightest upset could carry her off.

He picked up his bag, its weight adding to his guilty embarrassment.

"It is my custom to say a prayer for her," said his father, going down stiffly on his knees by the bedside.

"Yes, sir," Douglas's voice came out like that of an adolescent. The old lady's eyes opened briefly and twinkled a warning. "I'll say goodnight then, Mama." He lent over and kissed her, noting with satisfaction that the opium had nearly sent her to sleep. "Goodnight to you too, Father," he added and left.

PART III

THE PRODIGAL SON

*"For this my son was dead and is alive again,
he was lost and is found."*

St Luke Chapter 15, Verse 24

I

Early next morning, before the household was up, Douglas and Jean packed the money in the bottom of their big trunk, wrapping the gold coins in underclothes. To his amazement, his wife had not been shocked or even much surprised when he had whispered the story to her in the small hours of the night.

"She wants you to have it, Dougie. And whatever he may say, it's hers. That's how people think, nowadays. Ye aye telt me ma tocher belonged to me."

"I spent it, though."

"Aye, because I gie'ed it to ye. And when I've earned onything, like from ma bits of sewing and weaving, ye've never taken it from me."

"No. Because it should be yours. I love ye, Jeannie and I want you to have what is yours."

"I ken." Their arms tightened around each other. "And yer mother loves ye. She's made sacrifices for ye. That's why ye maun take what she's saved for ye."

"But . . . my father."

"There's no need to be scared o' him. He's just a puir auld man whose wife is dyin'."

"That's what he'd like ye to think."

"I'm thinkin' maybe he's a wee bit scared of *you*. For he sent for ye, and he canna do onything that'll upset her the now. He loves her ower much."

"Jean, he refused to let her doctor gie her painkillers

and she's suffering. Is that love?"

"Maybe now he's havin' second thoughts, and that's why we're here."

"I hope you're right."

Throughout the following day Douglas and his father succeeded in staying well-mannered toward each other. Mrs Stewart, refreshed by her good night's sleep, looked better. After breakfast Douglas carried her outdoors wrapped in a plaid, for the weather was warm and sunny.

The children ran around the Manse garden and played under her doting eye. Tommy, who loved animals, found a litter of kittens in a shed, and brought them out, one by one, for her inspection. Angus, growing bored, marched into the minister's study, something his father in his youth had never been allowed to do, and the Reverend Mr Stewart, instead of punishing the interruption, talked amiably with his grandson and showed him his books. When Rabb Innes came around for instructions, he slipped a small dark bottle into the doctor's hand.

At midday, Kenneth Stewart arrived with his wife, Effie, a plain, quiet countrywoman whom Jean liked. The couple had a little girl and a second child was noticably on the way. The two brothers, though they had never had many interests in common, had always enjoyed each other's company. Now, however, Kenneth's greatest curiosity seemed to be about how Douglas knew a 'Vicomtesse' well enough to stay with her in Edinburgh? Was she a patient and had he treated other eminent people?

"The rich can be sick just like us, Kenneth. I attend a' the gentry in Strathblane."

"Dougie cares for the puir too," said Jean. "And they only pay him in tatties and neeps or whatever they have."

"Very humanitarian of you, I am sure," remarked Mr Stewart who, Douglas observed, was taking advantage of the company and conversation to try and find out more about his eldest son's lifestyle, particularly his finances. The minister cross-questioned Kenneth about the economics of the wool trade, a profitable one these days in the Borders. The young farmer was growing affluent. He talked of building a new house and buying more land. He rode to hounds. He was active on the local political scene. Douglas sat back quietly, throwing in a few questions but offering little information about his own circumstances.

His children, however, were less restrained. Angus, who had had his grandfather's undivided attention until the little girl arrived, now started trying to get it back, through interrogating his cousin. Did she have a dog? He and Tommy had three, kittens too, and their Mama had a cow and hens. Did she go to school? A shy child, she hid bashfully behind her mother.

"Maybe you should tell us what kind of house *you* live in, Angus," said his Uncle Kenneth. "And what do you like to study at school?"

"Scripture. I'm goin' to be a minister when I grow up."

"Well! Well! A commendable ambition!" said Mr Stewart. He turned to Tommy. "And what about you, young man? What are you going to be?"

Douglas's second son, who had not previously received much notice from his grandfather, looked thoughtful, then stated, "I'm going to be a doctor like ma faither. A surgeon."

"Goodness me!" said Mr Stewart. "You must have a strong stomach. Could you cut people up? Take off someone's leg?"

Tommy considered this, then explained reasonably, "No the now, Grandfaither. But I'd gang to the university in Edinburgh and they'd train me."

His father grinned. "Well said, laddie!"

"Yes! Now tell us more about yourself, Dougie, and your medical career," said Kenneth. "Did you ever cut off a leg?"

"No, I'm glad to say I never had to. But of course I saw it done in the Medical School."

"He was asked to once," said Jean. "But he wouldna."

"Why not?" asked Mr Stewart. "Surely you were not squeamish?"

Douglas shook his head. He disliked this kind of conversation. It seldom came from any genuine desire to understand the problems doctors faced. It was simply curiosity. But they were all looking at him, expecting some response.

"My patient was a young farmer, about your age, Kenneth. He fell down a gully, going after a lamb. A colleague of mine, who is no surgeon, called me in, asked me to amputate the left leg, for on good medical grounds he believed this was necessary. I . . ." he shrugged. "I knew the man's circumstances. How could he manage, as a cripple? And so I decide I'd try to save the limb. I could always remove it later, after all."

They were listening, fascinated. "Surgery must be performed very fast, to spare the patient debilitating pain and shock, which can kill. But . . . I have become something of an expert in sedation." If he told them how Dr Franz Anton Mesmer used electric currents and animal magnetism to induce a trance, his father would accuse him of practising witchcraft, maybe even think he'd turned warlock. "I tried one of my methods on this man, and as he became less aware of the pain, I was able to take my time and put his leg back together. I'm glad to say it was most successful. He limps no worse than I do."

"Oh, Dougie!" exclaimed Mrs Stewart. "How wonderful! He must have been awful grateful to ye!"

"I hope you charged him plenty," said Kenneth.

"Ask my wife. She collects my fees."

"He paid what he could afford," said Jean. "But he was that happy, he gi'ed Dougie a nice wee mare as a present."

"Aye, I still have her, though she's old now and I make my rounds on a livelier horse. But sometimes, in an emergency, my apprentice still uses her."

"You have an apprentice?" Kenneth's tone was respectful. "You must have a very large practice."

"It's widespread. And he is now my partner since he just got his degree in Edinburgh."

"Dougie put him through the university," added Jean.

"No. I merely helped. He worked for his tuition, as I did. And he qualified in the nick of time to let me leave my patients in his hands and come here to see you." He turned to his sister-in-law. "Enough of this! Tell us more about spinning and weaving. Jean is an expert in both and she hopes to visit some of the woollen mills while she's in the Borders."

"I'll take her to see them!" said Kenneth. "I know them all."

In the evening, after the company departed, Douglas again carried his mother upstairs and once Jenny had settled her in bed, he got his bag, now emptied of the gold, and went in to settle her for the night. He had quietly given her a few sedatives during the day and had been glad to see she had been able to enjoy the party without undue strain or discomfort.

But now she did not argue when he measured the laudanum into her milk, although, as on the night before, she refused to drink it at once.

"Tell me how you put yourself through the Medical College, Dougie. I've so often wondered."

He told her how he had worked for Dr Tait and picked up money as an extra at the Theatre Royal, when Mrs Siddons' Shakespeare company came North on tour.

"So that's where you learned how to use your voice."

"Aye, watching the actors." He did not add that the actresses, one in particular, had also indoctrinated him into more carnal arts. "And a lady in Strathblane taught me to read musical scores. So I've been singing with a group that studied cantatas. But . . . I'm feared there will be no more of that now. She just died in childbirth."

"It was childbirth that started my problems," sighed Mrs Stewart. "All those dead bairns that came after Alasdair." The old satyr, thought Douglas, trying to keep her breeding when she was long past it. When the minister came in and cut short their conversation, his wife was again nearly asleep.

"There is a fair every Saturday in Melrose. Would you boys like to go to see it?" asked their grandfather at breakfast next morning. "And you must visit the ruins of the great Abbey. Your papa of course has seen it many times, but I am free enough today and I would enjoy telling you about its history."

Angus at least, was enthusiastic, but the prospect of a long walk didn't attract Tommy.

"You can come and go in the carriage," said Douglas. "The coachman is taking Jean to Melrose to meet Kenneth. He's escorting her around the wool mills."

The minister liked this idea and went off to make arrangements with Rabb. Jenny offered to care for Meg if her sister-in-law would do some marketing and errands at the Melrose fair, a regular source of supplies for the household.

"And how will you employ your time, son?" asked Mr Stewart.

"Since I came here to see my mother I'll be glad to spend a quiet day here."

After the sightseers left, Douglas, Jenny and their mother sat by the morning room fire and he told them about meeting Dr Peter van Buren and his wife's concert.

"Would you like to go to America, Dougie?" asked Mrs Stewart suddenly.

"Maybe. . ." Their eyes met. They were both thinking of the money under the spare bed.

Jenny giggled. "Don't say anything about that to Father! He disapproves of the colonists taking the law into their own hands and declaring their independence. He once caught me reading a book about America – Dr Matheson lent it to me – and I thought I'd never hear the end of it. But oh! I would love to see that wonderful country! Though I suppose I never will." She sighed and got up. "I must make soup for our dinner."

After Jenny went to the kitchen, Mrs Stewart said, "Now, Dougie, tell me more about how you trained your voice. I always wanted you to have singing lessons but of course your father wouldn't hear of it." When her son hesitated, she asked slyly, "Was it a woman who taught you?"

He nodded. "Sarah Siddon's understudy. She played Lady Macduff."

"And was she pretty?"

"Beautiful. She had wonderful long red hair. And she was a wonderful teacher – much better than any of the medical professors. She'd show me how the breath carried sound by holding my fingers to my ribs and my midriff so I'd feel the movement of the air while I spoke. And she'd recite Shakespeare – *Romeo and Juliet*, it was – and while I put my hands on her chest and her waist and. . ." He trailed off.

"Dougie, I think you're blushing. Did you fall in love with her?"

He got up, turned his back, walked over to the window. "Aye. Or so I thought, at the time."

"What became of her?"

"She went back to London with the players. She'd been born to the stage, her mother was an actress. She was ambitious. She'd never have been content as a country doctor's wife. Not that I could have married her then, anyway."

He fell silent, remembering things he had forced out of his mind for many years and could never tell his mother. Or anyone. "There was never another woman for me until I met Jean."

"You made a good choice in her, son."

"I know. I'm a lucky man. Mama, would you like a wee bit music?"

When she nodded, he sang softly:

Flow gently, Sweet Afton,
alang thy green braes.
Flow gently, I'll sing ye a song in thy praise.
My Mary's asleep by thy wandering stream.
Flow gently, sweet river,
disturb not her dream.

"Was Mary her name?"

"Aye. Mary McGuire." He shook off the memories. "Mama, let me tell you about my friend Paterson and how I got to know Jean when I was treating him for the wounds he'd suffered in France."

Later in the day, after Mrs Stewart had had her dinner and a nap, he acted out scenes from *Macbeth* for her. He knew the play by heart and his mother and sister were such a delighted audience he was in full histrionic flight when the carriage returned from Melrose.

"Continue! Continue!" exclaimed the minister, entering the room just as Birnum Wood was coming to Dunsinane, but his son fell silent.

II

At suppertime, Mr Stewart announced they must all go to bed early for the next day was Sunday.

"Do you attend the Kirk in Strathblane, Douglas?" he inquired.

"Yes, sir. So does my family."

"Are ye preachin', Grandfaither?" asked Angus expectantly.

"I am indeed, young man. Both in the morning and in the afternoon. And to that end, I must now make some preparations." He rose from the table. "You and Tommy had better go upstairs now, for we rise promptly and have prayers before breakfast."

"Aye and ye'll hae to put on yer new clothes that ye got in Edinburgh," said Jean.

Next morning, the two little boys, especially the elder, were so excited by the prospect of seeing their grandfather in the pulpit they submitted good-naturedly to being dressed up. They even tried to keep themselves clean as they knelt on the morning room floor while Mr Stewart read aloud from the Bible and prayed at length. But they were disappointed to find that they were getting a cold breakfast.

"Why are we no haein' porridge?" asked Tommy. "And it's gey chilly in here wi oot the fire!"

"It's the Sabbath," his grandfather reminded him. "The day of rest. Now drink your milk for shortly we leave for the Kirk."

At that moment, there was a loud tirling on the front door pin.

"Mercy!" exclaimed Jenny. "Whoever can that be? So early in the day. . ."

Her brother grinned at her across the table. "You would be used to unexpected visitors if you lived in a doctor's house."

"It's Mr Hogg, sir." The maidservant ushered in a skinny little man with such inflamed nostrils Douglas silently diagnosed a nasty cold.

"Mr Stewart, sir." The man's voice was a mere whisper. "I canna precent at the service. I'm awfu' sorry."

The minister looked unsympathetic. "You have left it somewhat late to advise me, Roderick. What of the other precentor?"

"He's away to Lauder. I was hopin' I'd be better the morn, but it's gone to ma throat. I'm losin' ma voice."

Mr Stewart rose from the breakfast table. "Well! Well! That is too bad." He smiled. "My son here is a physician. Perhaps he can to do something for you. This is Mr Hogg, Douglas, our schoolmaster and precentor. Can you suggest some treatment for him?"

"I have your permission to practise on the day of rest?"

"You have."

Douglas stood up, pushed back his cuffs, and assumed his professional manner. "Have you consulted your doctor, Mr Hogg?" The man shook his head. "No loss, for there is no cure for the common cold. It must run its course. But a bad throat can sometimes be helped. Jean, fetch me my bag, if you please."

"I'll get it for ye, Papa. I ken whaur it is." Tommy jumped up and rushed off upstairs.

Conscious of his father's eyes on him, Douglas did not wait for the sand-glass, but flipped open his watch and counted the man's pulse. Then, after a perfunctory examination of his patient's eyes and nose, he picked up a teaspoon from the breakfast table and rinsed it in a pitcher of water.

"Open your mouth as wide as you can, if you please. And try to relax. Now say *Ah*." An inarticulate croak emerged. Douglas depressed the man's tongue with the teaspoon which produced some gagging and spluttering. "You have a severe case of laryngitis, Mr Hogg, and resting your vocal chords is the only cure. Go straight home to bed and keep warm there for a day at least. And you must not open your mouth except to eat and to swallow plenty of liquids. No talking at all or you'll strain your throat."

"But," came a protesting whisper.

"Shh! You mustn't say a word. Not. One. Word. Understand?"

"Here's yer bag, Papa."

"Thank you, Tommy. Now let me give you a spoonful of cough syrup to ease the dryness." He measured it out and poured it down. "You can take this bottle home with you, for you'll need more of it. But the most important therapy is complete silence. And if you're not very much better in a couple of days, you had better send for me or for your own physician."

"But Mr Hogg is the dominie!" interjected Mr Stewart. "How can he instruct his pupils if you won't permit him to speak?"

Douglas picked up a table napkin and wiped off his hands. "Sir, you asked me to diagnose and prescribe and I have done so. In Strathblane we have an elder who takes the teacher's place if he is indisposed, and presumably you've some such arrangement in Darnick. But," he patted Mr Hogg's shoulder, "if you want this good man to make a fast recovery, he must rest his vocal chords. And tonight, sir, you should have a hot toddy, wi a good strong dram in it."

He took a couple of lemons from a dish on the sideboard. "Squeeze these into your drink." With his back to the company, he winked, and added softly, "Don't stint the whisky." His patient nodded, with a thin smile.

Douglas shook hands with him. "Take care of yourself, Mr Hogg. And remember, – No talking! Keep pen and paper beside you and write out anything you must communicate." He tugged at a plaid wrapped around the man's shoulders. "Cover your mouth against the cold and put on your bonnet before you go out. And don't worry. You'll feel better shortly, maybe even by tomorrow. But you must remain silent for a couple of days at least." He escorted his patient firmly to the front door and showed him out.

"Well!" said the minister. "What now? It's a quarter to ten and the first bell will be tolling shortly."

"My apologies, Father, but I did the only possible thing, medically speaking."

"I believe you, son. But what of the services? It was most inconsiderate of Mr Hogg to leave it so late before he informed me. Particularly with the other precentor away."

"He may well have thought he would be recovered. Laryngitis can come on unexpectedly in the run of a cold."

Angus was jumping up and down. "Dinna worry about the service, Grandfaither! Papa can be yer precentor. He does it in Strathblane."

Mr Stewart did not even try to hide his astonishment. "You act as precentor, son?"

Douglas said stiffly, "My children have been brought up to tell the truth." And the next time he had Angus alone he'd give him a good lecture on keeping his little mouth shut. "I precent if the dominie's sick."

"Other times, too," said Jean, proudly. "Mr Gardner, our minister, likes his voice, and the new sacred music he's learned."

"Then. . ."

"Then tell me which psalms you plan to use, Father, and the tunes you favour and I'll go with you to the Kirk."

"Oh Dougie!" exclaimed his mother. "I'd like to hear you! Do you think . . . ?"

"I'll sing them to you, later on, and perhaps. . ."

The minister interrupted, "Come with me to the study, son, where I have my notes."

Douglas had avoided that room. It held too many bad memories of tongue lashings and thrashings.

Then he remembered the money upstairs, and when he followed the minister into the library it was less threatening than he'd expected. The heavily stocked bookcases were still there, as were the uncomfortable chairs and the formidable desk, but the overall impression was darkness and stuffiness, unlike the sunny room in Strathblane where he saw his patients.

"You recall my order of service, son?"

"Refresh my memory. It may differ from what I am used to in the West."

"At the second bell, the congregation is admitted to the kirk and usually, although not today, I think, the precentor leads them in a psalm. By the third bell, I am in the pulpit. When I have greeted the heritors, I remove my hat and that is the signal for the singing to end. I then say a prayer. You return to the Manse pew as I start the Scriptural reading, and you stay there throughout the second prayer and my sermon. I have a sand-glass with me. When it runs out, I offer another prayer, and you then lead the second psalm before I pronounce the benediction. The order is the same at both services."

"So I'll need four psalms."

"Exactly. Do you have any preferences?"

"No."

Mr Stewart picked up a paper from his desk and handed it over. "Here is what I had planned for this morning. I presume you know *Dundee?*"

"I do. Isn't it a trifle short, if you have to greet heritors?"

"No, and I think that I had better mount the pulpit before the second bell, to introduce you to the congregation."

"Is that necessary?" His guts contracted.

"In the circumstances it would be appropriate. After all, why should the people follow the lead of a strange precentor?"

"True." They were almost talking like colleagues. "The second psalm, I see, is *Jesus shall reign*. Which tune do you favour? *Duke Street?*"

Mr Stewart displayed his remaining teeth. "That will give you an opportunity to show what you can do."

Douglas smiled back.

In the hall, Jean was ready with his hat. She had already put on her bonnet and wore her Paisley shawl.

"Are you coming with us, my dear?" asked her father-in-law.

"Aye. Jenny's following with Meg, after she's settled her mother. But the boys and I are going wi ye."

Angus and Tommy now wore little boys' suits bought in Edinburgh, a change from their childish dresses. Their shining hair was brushed, and their angelic expressions were too good to be true.

"Ye maun behave yersels now," warned their father, trying to look stern. "If ye dinna, I'll leather ye."

They had never been spanked, except in school, and

it was usually their mother who kept them in order at home.

"We'll be guid, Papa," they promised in chorus.

"If ye fidget, I'll take ye out before the sermon." That, he knew, would keep Angus quiet, and Tommy followed his brother's lead. The first bell started tolling as they entered through the back door of the old Kirk.

"You remember where to sit?" asked Mr Stewart.

"The pew to the right of the pulpit."

"Very good. Go and settle yourselves, and Douglas, be sure you have the aisle seat. I will signal to you when to rise and start singing. Here's the tuning fork."

"Keep it. I never use one. I've a good sense of pitch."

Douglas guided his family into the Manse pew, which, he realised, identified them immediately to the congregation. He recognised none of the people who were covertly eyeing him as they arrived and sat down. But villages being villages, there was undoubtedly plenty of gossip in circulation about his criminal past. His father, in a voluminous black Geneva gown, mounted the pulpit and stretched out both arms for attention.

"My friends," boomed the Reverend Mr Stewart. "We have a small departure from our usual order of service this morning. Mr Hogg is indisposed, and Mr Currie is away. However," his voice was all benevolence, "our precentor will be my eldest son Douglas, now visiting at the Manse. My son," he added unctuously, "who was lost and is found."

And, unlike the Prodigal, a successful professional man with a smartly dressed wife and three bonnie bairns. Douglas removed his hat, and stood up, smoothing down his hair and waistcoat, his gold watch and chain well in evidence. As he always did before precenting, he glanced quickly at his wife, who nodded. Secure in the knowledge that all was in place, he moved out and faced his father's congregation. He gave them a minute to gratify their curiosity, then filled his lungs and aimed his fine baritone at the back wall of the kirk, relieved to find he was in good voice:

> *Oh God of Bethel, by whose hand*
> *Thy people still are fed,*
> *Who through this weary pilgrimage*
> *Hast all our fathers led . . .*

By the end of the first verse, he had them following him as confidently as the people of Strathblane. Out of the corner of his eye, he was aware of Angus on tiptoes in the pew, the better to see his grandfather.

As the psalm ended, Douglas was reflecting that whatever natural force guided lives had done reasonably well by him. But God, the agnostic in him recalled, was alleged to help those who helped themselves.

After a lengthy prayer, the congregation seated themselves, and he was free to observe his father. It had been so long since he had seen him in the pulpit, he had forgotten the Reverend Thomas Stewart's impressive appearance up there. Like his firstborn, he stood over six feet tall and his thick white hair framed his handsome features dramatically. His gestures were sweeping, and he projected as melodious a voice as his son's.

So I inherited my most useful attribute from him, thought Douglas, and my lecturing ability too. His father delivered a remarkably informative sermon on the life of the Prophet Hosea, for which he must have done considerable research. And, unlike the good but prosy Mr Gardner, Mr Stewart could make the Biblical material seem relevant even to a congregation raised in the Age of Reason.

You should never see the legs of a minister, Douglas reflected. If I didn't know what an old bastard he was, I'd be filled with admiration.

The sand-glass ran out, Mr Stewart nodded impercep-
tibly and his son once more stepped out of the Manse pew
to launch into *Duke Street*, with Isaac Watt's words:

> *Jesus shall rein where e'er the sun*
> *Doth his successive journeys run . . .*

They sang all five verses. The minister pronounced the
benediction and the long service came to an end. Angus
had hung on his grandfather's every word and Tommy,
though he had yawned during the sermon, had kept still.
Jenny had joined them, bringing Meg who, as usual, slept
quietly.

In the church yard the congregation crowded around
the visitors and the minister's daughter made introductions.
Douglas was embarrassed because he had so little
recollection of the many people who greeted him by his
first name and claimed they had known him all his life. He
took refuge in smiling silence, and let his wife answer the
questions about when they had arrived, how long they
expected to stay, and how they liked the weather in the
Borders. All the villagers had admired the carriage, and
Rabb Innes, who had come to the service, also received his
share of attention.

When Mr Stewart came out, he showed off his
grandchildren with pride. Angus greeted the strangers with
a careful imitation of the minister's affable public manner.
Tommy held back, clinging to his father.

The crowd was thinning when a short well-dressed
man approached them, smiling. "I'm John Matheson, your
mother's physician. I graduated from the Edinburgh
Medical College two years after you did."

"Doctor Matheson. Did we ever meet?" Douglas held
out his hand.

"I don't think so but we all knew the famous Dougie
Stewart by sight!"

"Infamous, you mean." To his relief, it came out lightly.

"No! You were a great hero to your fellow students. You stood for what we all believed, in those days."

"Well, I hope you were warned by my fate to keep quiet about it. I'd like to talk to you. When would it be convenient? And not at the Manse."

"I'm home today. Why don't you come for supper and some refreshment after the second service? If you sing as magnificently as you did this morning, you'll need to wet your whistle."

"Thank you. Where do you live?"

"In the same house as my predecessor."

"A fine man and a fine doctor. He was a good friend to me." Douglas could not resist speaking up for the benefit of the minister, now within earshot. "And you must meet my son Thomas, who aspires to follow in our professional footsteps."

"How do you do, Thomas," said Dr Matheson as courteously as though addressing an adult. "Do you want to come with your papa this evening?"

Tommy looked up at his father who said, "I think he'd better go back to the Manse. Can you see the boys go home after the second service, Father?"

"Why, yes, I think I can be relied upon to take care of my grandsons."

Mr Stewart and the local doctor bowed politely, with nothing to say to one another.

"Douglas, we must hasten home for some sustenance. And we have to decide what you will sing this afternoon. Will you be with us at the afternoon service, Mr Matheson?"

The young man smiled. "If the music is as fine as it was this morning, it will be a pleasure." He tipped his hat.

"I'll see you later, Dr Stewart."

"I look forward to it. And since we were fellow students, why not call me Dougie?"

His father, he remembered, disliked his nickname.

"I've already heard that you were magnificent, son!" exclaimed Mrs Stewart, when they returned to the Manse. "Mrs Brown stopped by and so did Mrs Hogg. Oh, how I wish I could have been there! Perhaps this afternoon?"

"No, no, Margaret, you're not able." Mr Stewart was clearly more interested in his dinner of cold salmon and a mutton pie.

"But I am feeling so much better, these last few days, Thomas. Could I not go for the opening psalm and then slip out? I'm sure your parishioners would understand."

Before his father could refuse, Douglas pronounced, "A good idea. The short trip to the kirk will do you no harm." He was already working out how much laudanum would keep her comfortable and still leave her awake.

He poured himself a long glass of ale, for he was thirsty. "What do you want me to sing, Father?"

"Do you have any preferences?"

"No. But perhaps my mother has?"

"Oh, Dougie!" Her eyes filled with tears. "Would you sing the Twenty-third Psalm?"

"To the tune of *Crimond?*"

"Oh, yes, yes!"

"It has not yet been decided, Margaret, whether or not you should attend," said the minister. "Personally, I am dead against it. You haven't the strength."

"I can carry her to the kirk," said Douglas.

"And if I left after the psalm, the parish would understand. Oh, please, Thomas!"

"And how would you go home? It would be most improper for the precentor to leave."

"If I could find Rabb . . ." said her son.

"He's in the kitchen having a bite," contributed Jean. "He wants to go to both services, so . . ." she smiled at Jenny, "he was invited to come back here with us."

"Good. He won't drop you, Mama, he's very careful. Father, I wonder if you would like me to wind up with some modern music by that great composer, Haydn? In his oratorio, *The Creation*, there is a fine hymn which they enjoy in Strathblane. "He cleared his throat and carolled:

> *The spacious firmament on high*
> *With all the blue eternal sky*
> *And spangled heavens, a shining frame,*
> *Their great Original proclaim.*

"Oh, that's beautiful, Dougie!" cried his mother.

"Unsuitable. And unknown to our congregation," pronounced Mr Stewart. "I prefer *Old Hundreth*."

"Whatever you wish, sir."

"And the words will be the benedictory ones, *Praise God from whom all blessings flow*." A short, easy psalm with no opportunity for vocal pyrotechnics.

"I'll sing you the Haydn later, Mama," Douglas promised. "Though perhaps not tonight, for Dr Matheson has invited me to supper."

"Oh, I am so glad you have met. He is such a nice young man."

He stood up. "Now I'm going upstairs to prepare your bedtime medicine. Jean will put it in your milk. And I have a couple of pills that should give you strength to enjoy the service."

Mr Stewart bristled. "Do you, as a medical man, really believe she is able to go?"

"The weather is mild, sir. She is the better from fresh air and since she can leave whenever she feels tired, why not let her go to the kirk? Is she not entitled to worship God, if so inclined?"

A hard question for a minister to brush aside, and by the time Douglas had given Rabb directions, counted out some pills and measured the laudanum nightcap, it was time to leave for the afternoon service.

"We're comin' too, Papa!" announced Angus.

Tommy seemed less enthusiastic, so Douglas pocketed a handful of sweets from a jar in the morning room and noticing a little coil of string on the mantelpiece, he took that also, remembering how his mother had kept her young family amused through many a long sermon, playing cat's cradle with them in the Manse pew.

Jean and Jenny were wrapping a plaid around Mrs Stewart and covering her head with a warm bonnet, while Rabb, big and amiable, stood by ready to transport her.

"I trust you appreciate the gravity of the risk to your mother's health," said Mr Stewart, as he and his son walked over to the church.

Lowering his voice so that the children would not hear, Douglas answered, "Nothing will change the outcome of her illness. She might as well do whatever gives her pleasure."

"Well, on your own head be it, son. It's your responsibility."

"I'm accustomed to that kind of responsibility, Father."

The old man sniffed. "Yes. I suppose you are."

Inside the kirk, Douglas hustled his sons to the back of the pew explaining that their grandmother was to sit beside him on the aisle and they were to stay put when she left. As Rabb carried her in, with Jean at her side, a rustle went through the congregation and there were smiles and little waves of welcome. Jenny had stayed behind with Meg.

From the pulpit, Mr Stewart made no reference to his wife's presence, simply announced that, as in the morning, his son would act as precentor.

Douglas was nervous, but the actor in him responded. Earlier, he had simply sung. Now he projected more feeling than a precentor was supposed to do:

> *The Lord's my shepherd, I'll not want;*
> *He makes me down to lie*
> *In pastures green; he leadeth me*
> *The quiet waters by.*

> *My soul he doth restore again;*
> *And me to walk doth make*
> *Within the paths of righteousness*
> *E'en for his own name's sake.*

> *Yea, though I walk through death's dark vale*
> *Yet will I fear no ill,*
> *For thou art with me and thy rod*
> *And staff me comfort still.*

I'm with you too, Mama, he was telling her. I won't let you suffer at the end.

> *My table thou hast furnished*
> *In presence of my foes;*
> *My head thou dost with oil anoint,*
> *And my cup overflows.*

Consider that, you old windbag up there in the pulpit.

> *Goodness and mercy all my life*
> *Shall surely follow me;*
> *And in God's house for evermore*
> *My dwelling-place shall be.*

As the congregation rose for the prayer, Rabb gathered Mrs Stewart up in his arms and bore her out of the church, Jean at his heels. Someone else followed them quietly. Dr

Matheson. For the remainder of the service, Douglas had his work cut out to keep the little boys under control. Even Angus was restless by the end of the afternoon sermon. Tommy, when the sweeties were all gone, and he was tired of the string games, stretched out across his father's lap and went so soundly to sleep he was hard to ease off when the time came for the final psalm.

Again the congregation lingered after the service and crowded around Douglas, wanting to know about his mother. What did he think was wrong with her? Was her coming back to church after so many weeks a sign that she was recovering? Would she like her friends to call at the Manse? Could she go out for tea?

Evasive about the nature of her illness and its outcome, he staved off the well-meaning questions as he well knew how. He also fell back on the proper platitudes about Mrs Stewart's need for rest to discourage visitors who might overtax her strength. And he was adamant that he and his wife could not accept offers of hospitality since they would be in Darnick only a short time.

The socializing was easier than in the morning, for he felt a change in attitude towards himself. The village was accepting him as a respectable eldest son. Possibly his profession helped them to overlook his youthful fall from grace.

Still, he was relieved when his father emerged from the kirk and joined the company. Disregarding the many compliments paid to his son's singing, Mr Stewart again displayed his grandchildren, especially Angus who was basking in the attention and telling everyone he wanted to be a preacher when he grew up.

III

Dr Matheson had not returned to the service. His house was at the other end of the village and Douglas had some difficulty shaking off well-meaning but importune neighbours anxious to cross-question him alone about his mother's health. Eventually, he walked back to the Manse with his family, then went his own way from there. Darnick was a small village and he well remembered the shortcuts to the doctor's house.

His colleague opened the door himself and greeted him with, "You look in need of a drink."

"A correct diagnosis. What do you prescribe?"

"Whatever you please. Maybe whisky, in the circumstances?"

"You're a man after my own heart. Thank you for going back to the Manse with my mother. Was she very tired?"

"Yes, but stimulated and happy. I left her drinking tea and your wife was about to take the opportunity of the menfolk being away, to give her a bath downstairs by the fire."

"You mean someone had had the courage to light the fire? On the Sabbath? And in summer?"

"It was blazing happily and I suspect it was Jenny's doing. She's a sensible lassie, that sister of yours. She could be good looking, too, if she'd devote a little time to her appearance."

"Aye, that's true . . . John, isn't it? You're not married?"

"I was, but . . . she died in childbirth and the infant too. I am not yet recovered enough to go a-wooing again, although I suppose I will." He smiled as he handed Douglas a healthy tumbler of whisky. "When I do, I might include your sister among the prospective objects of my desire."

"You could certainly do worse. But could you stand your father-in-law?" They both laughed, toasting each other.

"I think," said Dr Matheson, "that if she accepted me, I would find it incumbent to move back to Edinburgh where I grew up."

"That might be wise." Douglas took a long pull on his drink. "Now tell me without preamble, how much time does she have?" They were not talking about Jenny.

"I'm amazed she has lasted this long. It was only the prospect of seeing you again, and your family, that pulled her through the last attack."

"It's cancer, isn't it?'

Dr Matheson nodded. "Have you examined her?"

"Only superficially. It's a little difficult, when she's your mother. But when I last saw her, over ten years ago, she was quite a well-covered woman. Now she's skin and bone. And I could feel the tumours even through her clothes. When did it start?"

"It's been coming on for a long time, I suspect. But the crisis came a few weeks ago. When I was called in, she was suffering so acutely. I gave her laudanum then went downstairs and told your father she was dying and it was only a matter of time. I confess I was flabbergasted by the way he behaved."

"He made a big irrational scene?"

"Exactly. He took his pain and anger out on me. Well, I'm used to that reaction to bad news. But then he forbade me to give her any more painkillers! Said she must be in her right mind to meet her Maker, though how she could be, in such distress, I don't know. And though I pled with him not to upset her, he rushed up to the bedroom, fell on his knees and begged her to go on living for his sake, offered to do anything for her, anything at all." Dr Matheson smiled. "And at that the old lady rallied and told him in no uncertain terms that he was to find *you* and bring you here."

"So that was what precipitated matters."

"Tell me, Douglas, how can I . . . how do you? . . . deal professionally with people like your father?"

"The unco' guid? In Strathblane I quote Scripture at them. They can't argue with the Good Book. Of course, being a son of the manse I'm well prepared with appropriate texts."

"A good idea. By the way, I was glad to find her pain seemed less acute and I won't ask how you achieved this. Do you need any more drugs?"

"I may need laudanum, shortly."

"Then let me give you some." He got up, took a bottle from a shelf behind his desk. "I'll put it with your hat in the hall."

"And charge it to my father."

"I will indeed. My housekeeper goes out each Sunday evening but she has left a meat pie, which is keeping warm in the kitchen. I hope you can join me?"

"Gladly. It will be the first hot food I've had all day."

"Then let's have it now." A trifle followed the pie and Douglas did justice to both.

"John, this is the first meal I've enjoyed since I came to Darnick. Just sitting at table with the old man gives me indigestion."

"D'you want something for that?"

"You've already given it to me." He raised the whisky glass. "And now tell me how the healing art is practised in the Borders! Have you done any engrafting against the smallpox?"

"Very little, though I believe in it."

"I met an American doctor in Edinburgh who told me our colleagues across the Atlantic are away ahead of us. In their War of Independence, they were treating whole regiments and their camp followers too."

"Ah, we're stuck in the mud here. The villagers are so afraid of anything new and none of the local gentry will give them a lead."

"I'm fortunate in having as a patient a Laird of a valetudinarian disposition. He married a charming widow in middle life and to everyone's surprise – including mine – she presented him with two offspring. Playing on his concern for their health, I persuaded him to order the Kirk Session to let me engraft the children in the parish school. He even disbursed the small cost of this foray into public health. I'm glad to say, it's been most successful. A number of the parents underwent the procedure at the same time and we've had no cases of smallpox in the valley all year." They settled down to a refreshing medical discussion.

But Douglas was tired and did not stay late. As he left, Dr Matheson asked, "If you're gone when the time comes . . . what do you want me to do?"

Their eyes met. Douglas, to his horror, found his own filling with tears. Finally he answered, "Do what I'd do if she wasn't my mother. Give her enough drugs to stop the pain and never mind the consequence."

It was still light and the air was gentle. Reluctant to return to the Manse, he strolled around the village, reflecting on how he had always loved the Borders and its people, some of whom he now encountered, also enjoying the balmy weather.

They greeted him in a friendly fashion, complimenting him on his singing, asking him where Strathblane lay in relation to Glasgow and how he liked living in the West. When they also made a point of telling him what a fine man his father was, what a magnificent preacher and what a kindly pastor, he smiled pleasantly and said nothing in reply.

IV

As Douglas approached the dark Manse, he saw with apprehension that there were still candles lit in the study and when he opened the front door, the minister called out, "Is that you, son?"

"Aye, it is."

"Come in here."

He felt the familiar contraction in his guts. "Yes, sir. As soon as I've seen to my mother." Upstairs, he left the bottle of laudanum by his own door, then went into Mrs Stewart's bedroom, where he was immediately aware of a change in the atmosphere. The aroma of sickness was gone, for all her bedding had been changed and she herself had been bathed. Even the strands of white hair escaping from under her nightcap were fresh and sweet smelling. She was also sound asleep so must have had her medicine. Douglas bent over her, felt her pulse, which was weak but steady, and kissed her gently. The old lady stirred, opened her eyes and murmured his name, and slept again.

Bracing himself, he went back downstairs and strode into the study. Without asking permission, he settled himself in the least uncomfortable chair and found a footstool to rest his weak leg.

"You've been drinking whisky," said Mr Stewart, sniffing the air.

"I have." And just enough to stimulate his mind. There could be worse times for a confrontation.

"It's the Sabbath."

"Aye. The day of rest and refreshment. Although both of us have worked hard. I enjoyed your sermons."

The minister made a noncommittal sound in his throat. "You were at Mr Matheson's, I presume. Did you discuss your mother's case?"

"Yes. And Doctor Matheson's diagnosis, alas, confirms my own. She has spreading cancerous tumours and there is no hope of recovery. She could go at any moment."

"She has appeared better these past few days. Last Sunday she could never have gone to the kirk, even briefly. Is not that a hopeful sign?"

"No. It simply indicates that when she has relief from pain she has more energy. I have been giving her opiates around the clock."

"I do not wish her to meet her Maker confused and in a drugged state."

"So you told my colleague." He took a deep breath. "When the soul abandons the body, it leaves behind the flesh and all it contains. That includes medication." Dubious thinking but it might offer the minister a rationalization.

The old man's voice quavered. "Is she suffering greatly?"

"Surely you can see that, sir."

"Yes. I have seen it. But it is the Cross she has to bear."

All the anger and disbelief he had experienced in his youth welled up in Douglas. He had heard that argument repeatedly when the childhood fever lamed him. It was what had made him an agnostic. But this was no time for theological argument. He had to hold his ground for his mother's sake.

"Your interpretation, sir, of the life of the Prophet

Hosea was most erudite and scholarly. I am sure you have an equally strong grasp of the teachings in the New Testament."

"I believe so, son."

"Then you will agree that, from all we know of him, the Christ was a merciful man who did everything he could to lessen the sufferings of others though he did not shrink from his own. As did his first disciples, the men who had known and worked with him. The Apostle Paul, too, that great evangelist, preached to the heathens a gospel of compassion."

The minister looked up in surprise. "We must do what is best for those we love. Sometimes it is necessary to be apparently cruel in order to be kind."

As you were to me, long ago, thought Douglas. He then quoted softly,

Though I speak with the tongues of men and of angels, and have not charity I am become as sounding brass, or a tinkling cymbal.

The sheer beauty of the words led him on.

And though I have the gift of prophesy and understand all mysteries and all knowledge; and though I have all faith, so that I could remove mountains, and have not charity, I am nothing.
And though I bestow all my goods to feed the poor, and though I give my body to be burned, and have not charity, it profiteth me nothing.
Charity suffereth long and is kind.

His voice, intensified by his breathing, underscored the last sentence.

After a pause, the minister asked, "You think I lack charity?"

His son didn't answer.

"I have acted for the benefit of her spiritual life. Her

soul. I regret her pain deeply." After another long silence, Mr Stewart added, "But you have expressed a powerful argument and, presumably, since it is your chosen profession, you know things that I do not about the end of life. You may continue to give her as much sedation as you think she needs."

Douglas restrained himself from replying that he planned to do that anyway. Having achieved his objective he had no more to say, and wanted to get away from his father as quickly as he could. He stood up, turning towards the door.

The minister raised a stern hand. "Do not go yet. I have not finished." Douglas turned cold with fear, as he had done in his boyhood.

"We too, Douglas Elliot, have unfinished business. Sit down." His son remained standing. He could not have moved. "I may have been over zealous in the way I treated you in your youth, but I believed then and still believe, that I was in the right. Certainly I made a man out of you."

I made a man out of myself, Douglas answered him silently.

"I trust you now understand that I simply meant to give you a stiff lesson in obedience when I turned you out. It was your own doing that you never came back. Certainly it was not what I then intended. I did not mean that you should abandon your home for good."

It didn't sound like that at the time.

"So I hope," Mr Stewart continued, his voice warming, "that you have long since forgiven and forgotten our unfortunate parting of the ways, these many years ago."

Isn't it enough that I'm here? thought Douglas. That I came back when you asked me? Must I also, like Macbeth, assume a virtue though I have it not and say *I forgive you, Father*?

And under the whisky's stimulation, he foresaw what was about to happen. The old man was building up a tearful reconciliation scene, a morally righteous one that would burden his son with lifelong guilt. It was how he had always disciplined his children. He had tried to stimulate their sense of shame, never appealed to them as rational individuals, even though, growing up in the Age of Reason, intelligence rather than sensibility was what his eldest son had always most respected.

Will he never learn? Douglas wondered. Can't he ever put himself in another person's shoes?

Then, in a flash of clarity, he realised that he himself could not change his own instinctive reaction either. By the way they were made, he and his father were predestined to rub each other the wrong way.

But I can't argue or contradict him and run the risk of a shouting match, Douglas raged on internally. And well he knows it, my old adversary who always hit me where I was most vulnerable. I must keep control of myself, for my mother's sake. I cannot argue with him, not even as a doctor. . .

Depression descended on him and with it came abysmal weariness. He hadn't the strength to cope with a replay of that terrible scene from the past, the regurgitation of old emotions. The strain of staying in that household had taken its toll on him. All his strength had been needed to control his own grief for the passing not only of his mother but of the man who represented the kind of wise, understanding parent the minister had never been. And on a deeper level he knew that, even to keep peace between them, he could never express to his father a forgiveness he did not feel. He so hated hypocrisy, he had trouble, despite his compassion, softening truth to reassure patients and their families even when his own feelings were not involved.

But it was urgent that he break the lengthening silence. The minister might burst into tears, lash out in anger as he had done at Dr Matheson, or rush upstairs to Mrs Stewart, now sleeping so peacefully. And when the uproar killed her, it would be his son's fault.

Douglas broke out in a chilly sweat. Throughout an eternity that was probably less than a minute, he stood tongue-tied, wishing he were back in Strathblane. And thought of the valley brought back Mr Gardner's words, *Love casteth out fear*. It was fear – old, childhood fear – that was paralysing him in mind and in body. Like stage fright, which, as a performer, he knew how to handle. He forced himself to breath steadily – in, out, in, out – and as he did so, his memory began to dredge up Biblical texts. In firm tones he said, "There is a Scriptural injunction, sir, that bids us judge not that we ourselves will not be judged."

And without waiting for a response, he strode out to the hall and picked up his candle. When he had, perforce, to return to the study to light it from the one on the minister's desk, he added rapidly, "Goodnight, Father. It has been a long day for both of us. Sleep well."

The old man, holding his head in his hands, was moaning tearfully, "Son, you are a better Christian than I am."

I'm not a Christian at all, Douglas thought, as he escaped upstairs to the safety of his wife's warm, welcoming arms.

"Dougie," she whispered, as he slipped, naked, into bed beside her, "she only needed half the medicine."

"How so?"

"I had it ready but she went to sleep fast. I'd washed her and given her a wee rub and she settled down like a baby. You doctors," Jean murmured fondling his cheek. "You're aye so free wi yer drugs."

V

Monday morning was so damp and grey the boys refused to play outdoors. They had the books and games provided for entertainment in the coach and Jenny supplied paper and drawing materials. But it was hard to keep them quiet and the minister emerged several times from his study, ordering them to make less noise.

Mrs Stewart did not get up, saying she was too tired and Douglas recognised a change in her. She sensed it herself. As he was taking her pulse, she said quietly, "The end's coming soon, is it not?" He met her eyes in silence. "I ken. And I'm ready. But, son, I don't want the bairns to be sad. They've enjoyed themselves here, haven't they?"

"They have that, Mama."

"Then, Dougie, I think you should go back to Edinburgh. Maybe not the day, it's ower late to start packing. But the morn or Wednesday."

Her eyes were dry but his were filling with tears again. "Mama, don't you want me beside you?"

"There's no more you can do, son. And he'll want me to himself. It's his right, he's my husband. . . You've made your peace with him, have you not?"

"I've . . . done the best I could. . ."

"He said you'd forgiven him. Telt me late last night, on his way to bed."

"Did he waken you?" The old bastard. Though it was a mercy the minister had interpreted the scene as he did.

"No. I was dosing and I slept again, never fear. But Dougie, do as I ask. Please."

He nodded. "Whatever you wish, Mama. I'll go and tell Jean."

"Aye, and send her in to me. I saved a piece of jewellery

for your wife if I ever saw her."

He found Jean downstairs, took her aside and told her the news.

"Ye think she'll die the day?" she asked.

"No. She's hung on this long, I think she'll wait until we're gone. But, ye never know. . ."

"Oh, Dougie." She put her arms around him. "It's unco' hard for ye. . ."

His eyes were filling again. "Not now, Jeannie." She held him tightly until he was back in control. "We maun do as she says. But we'll no tell the boys the day. Can ye pack without them suspecting?"

She smiled. "They're ower busy wi their ain pursuits. And wee Meg'll no notice. What about yer faither?"

"Mama will tell him . . . when she's ready."

Douglas spent the morning with his mother, talking to her when she was awake. He had given her extra laudanum although she did not seem in worse pain.

The minister, suspicious, lumbered upstairs and joined them. When he asked his wife if she would like him to pray she said yes. Douglas took the chance to go down and talk to his children.

"Your Granny's worse," he told them. "And ye maun be quiet. Very, very quiet. Understand?"

"Aye, Papa," they both assured him, and five minutes later were starting a fight.

Tension grew in the household. Jenny's solution was to bake, and she became so engrossed in the preparation of drop scones and crumpets, she neglected the midday meal. Usually, she had an imaginative hand for seasoning, but for that Monday dinner she served greasy tasteless underboiled mutton surrounded by overcooked greens. The two little boys pushed their food around on their plates until their mother ordered them sharply to eat it up.

"I dinna like it," said the uninhibited Angus. "Do *you* like it, Grandfaither?"

Mr Stewart said severely, "We must eat what is set before us whether we like it or not. It is good nourishing food and it must not go to waste."

Jenny, a little embarrassed, rose and went into the kitchen, returning with an apple tart fresh and fragrant from the oven. "Here's something you'll enjoy, laddies!"

"Oh goody, goody, goody!" exclaimed Tommy.

The minister's face darkened. "You will have no next course until your plates are clean. That has always been the rule in this household. Has it not, Douglas?"

His son knew that to his cost. "Aye. So you'd best eat up, boys."

Angus plunged resolutely into his food. But Tommy, though he managed to get down another mouthful of the mutton, dug his fork into the greens and left it there. "I canna thole it. . ."

"No clean plate, no pie," pronounced Mr Stewart. "Do you not have rules for the table, Douglas?"

"We do, but that is not one of them."

"Bairns must be taught obedience."

"True, but as a doctor, I have had to treat children who became sick when uncongenial foods were forced on them."

"But what we have here is nourishing and plain. Angus, you're a good boy. When your brother has followed your example, we will have the dessert."

Tommy forked a small quantity of spinach into his mouth, swallowed it, gagged, and turned to his father. "Papa . . . it scunners me."

It scunnered Douglas too, but he had to avoid a scene. "Tommy, if I ate your spinach, would you eat my tart?" The little boy's face lit up. "Then let us change plates.

Hand me yours." He cut up the unappetizing green mess on it and consumed it with apparent relish.

Before Mr Stewart could intervene, Tommy had demolished the apple pie.

Little Meg, usually so placid, began to sob. Jean picked her up and carried her off to bed. Mr Stewart rose, and so, thankfully, did the others. Glancing out of the window Douglas said, "The rain's stopped. Let's go for a walk, laddies, after I've looked in on Granny."

She was sleeping. Douglas found a pen, ink and paper on her bureau, and wrote quickly,

> *John, We are leaving tomorrow. You will know*
> *we are away when the coach is gone from the*
> *Inn yard. Please, then, come by to see my*
> *mother. Write to me at Blaerisk, Strathblane,*
> *in Stirlingshire. I appreciated your hospitality*
> *and the chance to talk with you. Yours aye, D.*

Pocketing this note, he went downstairs to find the minister had again retired to his study. Douglas rushed his sons out of the house.

"Where are we going, Papa?"

"First we're finding Rabb and then we're going to Dr Matheson's house. After that, we'll explore the peel tower."

At the Inn, he managed to brief the coachman without the boys overhearing the conversation. The doctor was out on a call, to Douglas's relief. After a prolonged scramble around the country roads and ruins, the children had worked off most of their energy and their father was also refreshed for he had enjoyed telling them stories about Border history. They were all in better spirits on their return to the Manse.

The minister, having had a quiet afternoon and possibly regretting his ill-temper at dinner, went out of his way to be charming to his grandchildren for the rest of the day. According to Jenny, he knew of their impending departure, though he said nothing about it.

That night, when Douglas went in to say goodnight, Mrs Stewart clung to his hand. "I'm scared, son. Stay with me, please. Even when I go to sleep. It's not right to ask you, when you've that long journey ahead of you, but. . ."

"Don't worry about me, Mama. I've sat up through many a night with patients, and with Jean when she was in labour."

"Oh, Dougie, there's still so much you have to tell me about your life!"

"Mama, there are things I should ask you too."

"I know. About your future." She pressed his hand. "Dougie, go across the seas. You've ower much ambition to be satisfied in a wee country like Scotland. And, don't wait too long. . . "

As the laudanum quieted her, he settled himself in a small chair, which he moved to the other side of the bed when his father came in. While the old man was there, praying and talking softly to her, Douglas closed his eyes and tried to nap. But he slept little, alert to every subtle change in her breathing.

She was still alive when morning came, though perceptibly weaker. After breakfast, Rabb arrived with the carriage and loaded the heavy trunk into the boot. Jean, somehow, had packed all that had been in it before into bags. Taken by surprise but sensing the gravity, the boys rose to the occasion. When they were dressed, their mother took them to their grandmother's room. She kissed them, gave each one a small present, and some old toys of their father's. Jean, misty-eyed, hugged her then followed her family downstairs, leaving mother and son alone. For only a few more minutes would he have to be strong. She held out her arms and they clung to each other until she whispered, "Now go, son. And the Lord go with you. . ."

"Mama . . . all those years, I felt you at ma side. . ."

"I was there, Dougie, and I'll still be there. . ."

Outside her door, he blew his nose, mopped his face, forced over his emotion the facade of the medical man. In the hall, well in control, he gave some coins to the little servant girl, thanked her for her efforts, kissed his tearful sister. Then he faced his father. And, as a physician, he no longer saw a tyrant and bully but an aging, grief-stricken man on the brink of terrible loneliness. He had had to comfort many such and now he acted as he always did. He set his big reassuring hands on the minister's shoulders, pressed them hard and looked into his eyes with genuine compassion.

Mr Stewart clutched his son to his bosom. He sought words but he was too choked by his tears. All he could do was blurt out, "Dougie . . . yer singin' was fair beautiful. . ."

Disengaging himself, Douglas fled down the path to the carriage, thankful they would never meet again.

"I must show Ralph the way to Melrose," he called to Jean as he clambered up beside the coachman, and motioned him to start.

"Wait, sir! Wait! Miss Stewart's callin' ye."

Jenny had run after him. "Dougie, you forgot your hat."

As he leaned down to take it from her, she said, "Let me go to America with you! I'll work! I'd not be a burden! I'll help Jean with the children! Please, Dougie!"

He nodded. Rabb shook the reins, and the carriage rolled off down the road.

As they reached the outskirts of Darnick, the coachman freed one hand, dug in his coat pocket and pulled out a bottle. "I got ye a replacement, doctor."

Douglas had never even opened the first pint of

whisky. But now, he pulled the cork, swallowed a long comforting drink and offered the flask to his companion.

"No thank ye, sir, no while I'm drivin' the nags, but later, maybe."

"I appreciate this, Rabb. I'm telling Mr Paterson, once we're home, how well ye've cared for us all." And Strathblane was home now. At least, for the present.

Once again, they stopped on the top of Soutra Brae. Jenny's picnic was not as fancy as Clementina's but just as acceptable to the children. Neither Jean nor Douglas could eat. The sun was shining but the wind was so cold they did not want to linger. When Douglas wandered off behind some bushes, Tommy followed him.

"Papa, can I ask ye a question?"

"Aye, what is it?"

"Is Grandma goin' to die?"

"We're all goin' to die some day."

"Aye, but soon?"

Douglas looked down at him. "What makes ye think that, laddie?"

The little boy wrinkled his forehead. "Ye mind yon old lady – Mrs Taggart – in Strathblane? I used to go in after school and feed her pussies for her. The day she died, she'd the same look Grandma had this morn."

"Tommy, when you're a doctor, you'll be strong on diagnosis."

"Thank you, Papa." He thought about this and asked, "What's *die-a-noses* mean?"

"*Di-ag-nosis*. It means that while you're examining your patients you're noticing whatever isn't as usual with them, and from those things – which may be quite small – you gain information. And from that you deduce what may be wrong. Understand?"

"I think so. What may be wrong. Papa. . . ?"

"Aye?" But Tommy thought better than to ask the other question on his mind, and changed his request to, "Can I gie yin o' ma wee picture books to Anne?"

"Anne?"

"Anne Paterson. I telt her I'd bring her a present."

"Aye, that would be nice."

"I'm going to marry her when I grow up." Tommy explained.

Walter Paterson's pampered daughter was unlikely to take a country doctor's son as her bridegroom. "Ye'll need to earn a lot of siller first."

"Oh, but I will, Papa." The childish voice was confident. "I'll be a surgeon. And every time ye come hame after ye've done an operation ye tell Mama surgery is where the money is."

For the first time since he'd left Edinburgh, Douglas's laughter was real.

PART IV

NEW PEOPLE, NEW PLACES

Had I plenty of money, money enough to spare,
The house for me, no doubt, were a house in the city square.
Ah, such a life, such a life, as one leads at the window there!
. . . The city, oh the city – the square with the houses! Why?
They are stonefaced, white as a curd,
                          there's something to take the eye!
Houses in four straight lines, not a single front awry.
                          Robert Browning (1812–1889)
                          Up at a Villa, Down in the City

I

Clementina's warm welcome, and the luxury of the Charlotte Square house soothed the exhausted Stewarts. Even so, Douglas could not sleep the night they arrived. He was worrying that Dr Matheson might not have understood his note. He also kept thinking up questions for Peter van Buren.

Jean too was restless and in the morning, she jumped up hastily from the breakfast table and rushed back to the bedroom where Douglas, following, found her vomiting into the water basin.

"Jeannie! What's wrong?"

She raised baleful eyes to his. "Ye ca' yersel a doctor and ye need to ask, what's wrong? when yer wife gets sick in the morning?"

"Good God! Are ye breedin' again?" That could complicate the immediate future.

She burst into tears. "Aye. I've been doin' this a' week but – I managed to hide it – ye'd ower much to thole."

"Jeannie, I'm delighted! Anither wee Stewart! I only wish Mama . . ."

"I telt her, Dougie. She was fair pleased."

"Oh, ma dearie. . ." He hugged her, then remarked, "So I'm the last to know."

She shook her head. "I only telt yer mother. But I think Tommy suspects. He caught me cleanin' masel up yesterday morn."

"He's observant, that wee character." He wiped her face with a towel, fondling her hair. "Now come back and replace the nourishment ye just lost."

"Oh no, Dougie!"

"Oh yes, Jean!" said Clementina from the doorway. "I don't mean to be nosy or interfering, but I knew. I wasn't long past that stage myself when you were last here, but now I feel fine and so will you. Very soon, too."

She took Jean's arm and led her back to the morning room.

"But, to hae it happen the now, when I was so lookin' forward to seein' Edinburgh!"

"You will! You'll feel better in a wee while. Until tomorrow morning." She poured tea. "Now drink that up and remember it'll stay down this time. You've gone through this before."

"Aye, but it never gets any easier."

Over Jean's head, Clementina signalled to Douglas to make himself scarce. He said, "I'll go find Rabb and see where he plans to take the boys."

But that had already been decided. "Angus wants to see John Knox's house, Doctor, and then we maun visit St Giles Cathedral and the Grassmarket where a' the Covenanters glorified God and died." The coachman grinned. "He got a fair dose o' religious instruction from his grandfaither."

"Aye. More than he ever got from me. What about Tommy?"

"Tommy wants to see the Infirmary."

"No. Absolutely not. Sights not fit for a sensitive wee laddie. But take him by the building, then show him the University and the Medical College." Douglas handed over some cash. "Here. That's for the whisky, and maybe ye'll want to stop off at a pub at midday. Introduce the boys to

Luckie Ferguson's, or wherever the students go these days."

Back in the morning room, the two young women were happily planning their day and Jean was nibbling an oatcake.

"Clementina," Douglas said, "you're a banker's daughter. Maybe you can give me some advice. I brought a large sum of money back with me from Darnick, in cash and I'm nervous about travelling home with it, in case we meet highwaymen or stop off at an inn and are robbed."

The Vicomtesse nodded. "Jean told me. There should be no difficulty. We'll take it over to the Royal Bank in my carriage. I know the manager well and you won't need to explain anything. Banks always accept deposits. And they can arrange for it to be credited to your account in Glasgow. You do have one there, don't you?"

"Aye," said Jean. "For our savings." And pretty meagre these had been until now.

"After the children leave, we'll go." Clementina added, "Better not say anything to Rabb. I know he's discreet, but he might tell his wife once he's home."

"Aye, and it'd be a' over the village that Dougie had come into an inheritance. Ye're right, Clemmie. Whatever would we do wi out ye?"

"You'd do very well. And after we've been to the Bank, you and I are going sightseeing."

"Have you news of Dr Tait?" asked Douglas.

"Oh. You hadn't heard? He died the day after you saw him."

His heart sank.

"Dr van Buren came by to tell you. He thought you might still be here. And he left a letter. He's very anxious to see you. I told him as soon as you returned, he and his wife must join us for supper, and I've already sent a footman to his house inviting them for tomorrow. Would you like me to ask Dr and Mrs Gifford too?"

"Clemmie, you overwhelm me."

She smiled at him, "Well, you did save my brother's life, you and Jean. Now let me go and find valises for your money and we'll be off." She went to a little desk, picked up a folded sheet of paper. "Here's what Dr van Buren left for you."

Douglas opened it, and caught his breath when he saw Dr Tait's writing.

"My dear Dougie," the old man had scrawled. "Go with Peter to New York and God bless. A.Tait."

"I suppose," he swallowed, "they've already had the funeral?"

"Yes. A big service in St Giles. But if you want to find Dr van Buren, I imagine he'll be at Dr Tait's house. And if not, here's his home address." Clementina scribbled a note and handed it over. "If they're engaged tomorrow, tell them to come tonight, though you might like to have an early evening. Besides, my father may stop by. He's staying with my uncle, while Mama's in Strathblane." She smiled. "I did tell you, didn't I, that she'd gone to help my poor brother with his household? And she's taken Betsy with her."

"Betsy?" queried Jean. "Who's she?"

"Our cousin. She was very sweet on Walter once, and I think he liked her but of course he'd already fallen in love with Primrose."

"And this Betsy never married anyone else?"

"She was engaged to a young man but he joined the Navy and was killed in the engagement at Aboukir Bay."

"That was some time ago," remarked Douglas.

"Yes, but so many eligible men have gone off to war. . . Betsy's very clever. She's edited books for an Edinburgh publisher. That should make her useful to Walter. He said in his last letter he was worried about a manuscript he had to complete."

"Is she pretty?" he asked. There was, after all, more to making a match, as this project clearly was, than working on literary affairs.

"Well, she's handsome, but of course, she's thirty. You'll meet her when you go back to Strathblane. She'll be staying on after Mama returns home."

"Is she good wi children?" asked Jean.

"She likes to play with mine and show them off when she takes them out walking."

A little different from handling three motherless bairns, two of them old enough to feel their loss, thought the doctor.

As Clementina had forecast, there were no problems at the Royal Bank. Indeed, the amount of money commanded such respect, the Manager poured Douglas a glass of claret while he was completing a proposal form for the deposit, giving information on where and when he might wish to avail himself of the funds. Then the bundles of notes and the gold coins had to be counted and the paperwork of transferring the money to Glasgow completed and signed.

Clementina, after introducing the Royal Bank officials, had returned to her carriage to wait with Jean. When he eventually joined them, his wife asked, "Do we hae enough to go to America?"

He nodded. "More than enough. And meanwhile I want you to buy some bonnets and trinkets." He handed her ten pounds.

"Dougie! That's far too much!"

"You've earned it, my dearie."

"And I'll make sure she spends it all on herself!" said Clementina. "Now where can we take you, Douglas?"

"To Dr Tait's house, if you please."

There, as he'd expected, he found Peter van Buren in working clothes sorting and packing up the professor's books and medical paraphernalia, all willed to the Medical College.

Without waiting to be asked, Douglas peeled off his coat, rolled up his sleeves, and lent a hand. It was a back-wrenching and emotionally distressing job, but the two young men found plenty to discuss. They continued their conversation over a meal at the ordinary then visited the Infirmary.

When Douglas brought up the possibility of moving to America, he found his new friend had already been considering the idea and had talked it over with Dr Tait, who had strongly approved.

"The old man thought you and I would get along, Doug," said Peter van Buren. "And we sure need properly qualified medical men in the United States. The country's growing fast."

"Plenty of patients for everyone, eh?"

"Exactly. And the future isn't as settled as it is in Scotland. I mean, if we went into partnership but you found you preferred practising on your own, it would not be hard for us to go our separate ways."

"And if you decided to kick me out or I didn't like New York, there would be plenty of places for me to go?"

"Sure. There's Philadelphia, if you wanted to teach. And territories out West, still unexplored."

"That doesn't attract me, though Jean likes the country, and I'm a bit concerned about how she'll take to living in a city. I prefer 'em, of course, preferably with theatres and concerts."

"Then you should stay in the East and of course Johanna and I think there's no place like New York.

Boston's a nice town, too, and full of culture, but it's perishingly cold in winter."

Douglas hesitated, then said, "I presume you have heard how I was once a jailbird and publicly chastised here in Edinburgh?"

Peter van Buren laughed. "Oh yes! And branded as a felon. But no-one cares in the United States. When we were separating ourselves from King George, many people went to prison for political reasons – and your brush with the law was just that, according to Dr Tait. He talked of you so much I feel I know you well. And," he added, "I have drawn my own conclusions about Dr Baxter. I would not want to have him for an enemy in a small country like Scotland."

Over a quiet supper at Charlotte Square, Douglas told his wife and Clementina about this conversation and how, later that day, he had also made some inquiries about requirements for emigration to the United States.

"But how exciting!" cried the Vicomtesse. "Louis and I talked about going to America when we left France. But with all my family here, Edinburgh seemed a better place to settle."

"Aye, and ye're acting as though it's a' decided, Dougie. Does yer wife no hae ony say in the matter?"

"Of course she does. You know that. But . . ." And then he remembered she was pregnant. "Jeannie, we don't have to leave right away."

She gave him a straight look. "But we're goin' to America, that's what ye mean. We're no biding here in Scotland."

He nodded.

"Well, tomorrow night you can ask Mrs van Buren all about New York," said Clementina. "And I told her to bring her music, so we can have a little concert. The

Giffords are coming too." And with that, she chased the Stewarts off to bed, where they lay side by side in unaccustomed silence, again unable to sleep.

II

Next morning, Douglas went back to Dr Tait's house but most of the clearing was done and Peter van Buren had patients to visit. So they went their separate ways, knowing they would meet that evening.

Douglas walked around Edinburgh, revisiting old haunts. It might, after all, be the last time he would see the beloved city where he had first lived on his own, making his own decisions, and where he had discovered so many new talents, like singing, to say nothing of his vocation.

But the Capital had changed or he had, more likely. Now he was conscious of the dirt and disease in the Old Town, its poverty and overpopulation. He no longer wanted to practise there, or even in the New Town, for the uniformity of the terraces suggested a closed society with shared values. There might be stimulating personalities like Mr Walter Scott among the legal and literary fraternity, but Douglas wondered about the medical establishment where, after all, he belonged.

Then a small unpleasant incident happened. He had been walking past the Surgeon's Hall, debating whether or not to go in and seek out some old acquaintances, when Dr David Baxter came through the door accompanied by a group of young men to whom he was expounding on some professional topic. Douglas gave him a civil nod of recognition, but that wasn't enough for his old enemy.

"Ah! Dougie! How does it feel to walk the streets of Edinburgh as a free man?" He turned to his entourage.

"This, gentlemen, is a former classmate of mine, Dr Douglas Stewart. You may have heard tell of him. A political rebel. They flogged him outside the Tolbooth for his youthful indiscretions and he went off to practise in the wilds of the West."

Douglas felt his face flame. But he contrived to smile and respond pleasantly. "I perceive you still carry a scar on your forehead, Davie, from our last fight in our cups. I knocked you flat on your face. For which you turned me over to the authorities as a dangerous Radical." He turned to the students and added, "Watch out for him, gentlemen, he has a long memory." And, tipping his hat, he strolled on.

But the day had been spoiled. He had walked and walked, in and out and up and down through the wynds of the Old Town, until his rage had cooled. But when the clouding sky forecast a change in the sunny weather, he headed back to Charlotte Square.

The footman who let him in said, "Sir, your coachman would like a word with you."

Douglas's heart sank. "What's happened? My children?"

"They're playing in the park with Master Pierre and Master Gérard. The nursemaid's keepin' an eye on them. And the ladies are still out shopping. Would you like me to show you the way to the stables?"

"If you please." As they went through the basement towards the outbuildings, Douglas had his first chance to see the amenities of the house, including the fine modern kitchen which had so impressed his wife. It impressed him too.

The Strathblane horses were in comfortable stalls off a back lane but their coachman looked so perturbed the doctor asked, "What's the matter, Rabb?"

"Maybe nothing, sir, but I'd like to hae your opinion on Hannibal."

"Why?"

"He's just no hissel, the day."

Douglas went over to the horse's stall, patted the animal, prodded him here and there, and contrived to take a quick look into his mouth. "I can't see anything wrong. Why are you worried?"

"Ach, maybe it's just that he's old. Mr Paterson did say to me, when we were leaving Strathblane, that this might be his last long trip."

"Aye, horses age, like the rest of us."

"They do that, Doctor."

"D'you think he's fit for the return journey?"

"Oh aye, sir. But, I was wondering . . . It's longer to go by way of Glasgow, but the roads are better and there's no that many hills to climb."

"And there's that good horse doctor in the Broomie-law."

"Aye. If we were to stop over, he could tak' a look at Hannibal."

"A good idea. I see no reason why we can't spend a night in the town. But of course, I'll have to talk it over with my wife."

"When were ye planning to leave, sir?"

Douglas shrugged. "In a couple of days, maybe sooner. But surely Madame de Sincerbeaux has a veterinary expert for her horses? Have you asked?"

"Aye, I already took the liberty, sir, and he came around the morn. Like you, he found nothing wrong. But he did say Hannibal needed a rest."

"Then he shall have one." Douglas patted the old horse. "And we can spend two nights in Glasgow, if need be. I have to restock my medical supplies. Dr MacLean and I can always use more leeches."

He could also find out more about emigration permits and sailings, and make sure the money was in his account at the Royal Bank.

Jean, when he told her, approved of this break in their journey home. "We could sleep over at ma cousin Willie's." She pointed out, "He's got a big house, and it doesna inconvenience his wife since they've no children."

Douglas groaned. "Willie MacDougal is the most boring man I ever met! Why don't we stay at an inn? We can afford it now."

"Aye, but he owes us some hospitality. We aye gie him guid meals when he comes to Strathblane to visit his factory." She hesitated then added, "Dougie, Willie has ships going and coming from America. Ye could talk to him about sailings."

So she had accepted the idea. "Why don't you write him a note today and say we're coming to dinner on – whatever day we decide to leave. For myself," he remarked, "I'm ready to go as soon as Hannibal is rested."

Clementina's supper party was lively and enjoyable. It also reinforced Douglas's impressions about his profession in Edinburgh. While the Vicomtesse took her female guests to the nursery to see the children, the men had some professional discussion.

Bob Gifford, the fashionable Edinburgh physician, was not interested in the lively medical arguments Douglas and Peter immediately got into, first on the subject of engrafting against the smallpox, and then on Mesmerism and the usefulness of animal magnetism in surgery.

"Dougie! You mean to say you're still experimenting with that trance nonsense!" exclaimed Dr Gifford.

"I'm no longer experimenting, I'm availing myself of the procedure. I still don't understand how it works but that's beside the point. I can perform operations that otherwise I wouldn't risk, and I've been very successful. My patients have recovered admirably and with no bad memories of their ordeal."

"How did you learn of this magnetism?" asked Peter.

"From a French doctor, a refugee here in Edinburgh that I met in my student days. And Bob, you were as intrigued as I was when he showed us how he could control pain. Remember when I had that tooth pulled and felt nothing? And you were good at it! Why did you give it up?"

Dr Gifford shrugged his well-tailored shoulders. "I found it was a little too esoteric for my patients. People here are pretty conservative these days."

"That's not what you told me the other night. You said the town had become extremely liberal!"

"Well, yes, politically, but our profession's different. I gave up inducing trances when one of my colleagues – I think it was Davey Baxter – started spreading gossip that I was dabbling in sorcery and the black arts."

"In America, we're frankly fascinated by sorcery," said Peter van Buren. "Ever hear of the Salem witches? Tell me more about this talent of yours, Douglas."

"You're not scared of it?"

"I'm not scared of anything to do with electricity. I've been intrigued by its medical possibilities ever since I heard old Ben Franklin talking about it."

"Aye. Dr Tait met him, when he was in Edinburgh, said he was one of the most scientifically curious men he ever knew. Is curiosity typical of Americans?"

"I think so. Here in Edinburgh, people accuse me of asking an awful lot of nosy questions."

Later, they joined the ladies in the drawing room and had some music. Peter played the violin reasonably well.

Bob Gifford had brought his oboe. Douglas sang. They performed Haydn and Mozart and Handel, then drifted into the popular songs of Robert Burns.

"Oh, my! We need you in New York, Dr Stewart!" exclaimed Johanna, who had been accompanying them on Clementina's grand piano. "I have a choral group, and I always need good baritones."

"That settles it, partner!" said her husband, grinning at Douglas. "You'll have to move to Manhattan or I'll never hear the end of it!"

"And, as a singer," went on Johanna, "you must know a great deal about treating the throat."

Douglas nodded. "I confess I've always had a personal interest in it, and diseases of the chest too, like consumption."

"In New York, there are many actors and singers."

"And all of them hypochondriacs," added Peter, "so between performers and the Dutch community to whom I'll introduce you, you'd find plenty of work as a chest and throat specialist. Which I'm not."

"And now that the French War is well over we expect we'll have more touring companies from Britain and Europe," said Johanna.

"The war isn't *well over*, I'm afraid," said Clementina. "I had a long letter from my husband today. He's still in Paris, but says he's cutting his trip short because he's afraid this Peace of Amiens is just a brief pause in hostilities. He can't wait to get our little son safely back to Scotland, and he just wishes he could persuade his parents to come too."

"Is it this man Napoleon Bonaparte, who's stirring up the trouble?" asked Bob Gifford.

"Yes. Louis says he's terribly ambitious, and plans to conquer the whole world. And he's already created a very efficient army."

"So maybe we'd better not go to Europe, Peter" said Johanna.

"I thought you were about to return to America?" Douglas queried.

"We are," Peter answered. "Now that Dr Tait's gone, I don't want to stay in Edinburgh. In fact, this afternoon, I went down to Leith to find out about sailings. But neither Johanna or I have ever been to Holland. We both have relatives there and we may never be in this part of the world again, it's such a long way from America. So we'd like to visit the Netherlands before we go home."

"But we must cross the Atlantic before the hurricane season starts," Johanna smiled. "And I'd like to be back in New York in time to enjoy the Indian Summer. Do you like hot weather?" she asked Jean.

"No as much as Dougie. He loves it."

"So do I," said Dr van Buren. "After two winters in Edinburgh, I never wanted to feel that damp Scottish chill again. Besides, we keep our houses warmer in the United States, at least in the North."

"Isn't that unhealthy?" asked Bob Gifford. "Doesn't it make people soft?"

Peter van Buren just shook his head.

III

Next morning, while Jean and Clementina were dressing for another shopping expedition and Douglas was reading the newspaper over a leisurely cup of *cafe au lait*, the butler came into the morning room.

"Dr Stewart, sir, there is a young man at the door who says he is your brother and he wishes to see you. Shall I admit him?"

"Oh, mercy!" He had completely forgotten about Alasdair. "Yes! Bring him in."

His conscience stirring guiltily, Douglas hurried out to the hall, where a shabby youth stood twisting his hat in his hands under the watchful eye of a footman. The brothers could have passed each other on the street without recognition. Alasdair was small and fairhaired and the only family resemblance was in his eyes, which were heart-rendingly reminiscent of their mother. The visitor, for his part, was looking at the big, confident, well-dressed man now approaching him as though he could not believe who he was.

"Alasdair! What a welcome surprise!" Douglas started to hold out his hand, then put his arms around his sibling and hugged him. "I was about to call on you today at your lodgings." That was true in intent at least.

"Dougie! Oh Dougie! Mama's dead!" The young man burst into tears. "I had a letter from Father. She's gone!"

"When?"

"The day you left Darnick. He wrote to me at once, caught the afternoon mail coach. He said I'd find you here, and to tell you. . ." He was extending a crumpled paper.

So John Matheson had followed directives. Douglas swallowed. Though he had expected the news it still hit him hard. In silence, he led his brother into the morning room and as they passed the sideboard, picked up a decanter.

"Have a dram, laddie. You're shivering." He poured two shots of whisky.

"Oh, no, Dougie! I couldn't drink that! It's too strong!"

"It's what we need." He emptied his own glass in one gulp.

Alasdair risked a sip and then another, but he seemed

more interested in the cut glass tumbler and his eyes, roaming over the elegant room, lingered on the covered silver serving platters on the buffet table. "I've had no food the day. Could I maybe have something to eat?"

"Anything you like. Help yourself. Set another place at the table," Douglas ordered the footman, who obeyed him smartly and poured Alasdair some coffee. "Now tell me about Mama."

"It's all in that letter."

Douglas strode over to the window, turning his back as he opened the minister's terse communication. Mrs Stewart had slept peacefully away after a visit from her physician who had come to the Manse almost as soon as the Strathblane carriage left.

"Dougie. . ."

"Eat your breakfast, laddie, and then we'll talk. . ." He was staring out at Charlotte Square, tears running down his cheeks, his hands shaking.

"Dougie, how d'you come to be staying in such a grand house?"

"It belongs to the sister of one of my patients. She married a rich Frenchman." At least he could control his voice.

In silence, Alasdair demolished a quantity of bacon and bannock, then asked, "Can I travel back with you?"

"Back . . . where?"

"To Darnick. Are you not going home?"

Douglas reached for a table napkin and wiped off his face. "Strathblane is my home now, laddie."

"But . . . Mama's burial . . ."

I couldn't bear it, he thought . . . a long cold funeral service, then that old hypocrite, who let her suffer so grievously, crying over her open grave. "They'll have buried her by now."

"But . . . Father . . . He'll want his children. . ."

"He'll have all but me. Tell him I have professional commitments. I'm a physician as maybe you know."

Alasdair nodded. Again surveying the luxurious surroundings he said in whiney tones, "Dougie, I've no enough money for the stagecoach. Not even to go with the mail. Unless you help me, I'll have to walk all the way."

His brother was shocked. "You can't. It's around forty miles."

"I've done it before at the end of the term."

I never did, thought Douglas. But of course, I was lame in those days. "Does Father keep you that short of cash?" He felt another twinge of guilt.

"He says he gives me all he can spare. By the time I've paid for my lodgings and my tuition I've scarce enough left even for books and food."

"Don't you work as well as study? I did. I cleaned up laboratories for my professors. And I was an extra at the Royal Theatre. You're nice-looking, you could earn good money on the stage."

It was Alasdair's turn to be horrified. "Oh no, Dougie! I'm studying for the ministry. I never go to plays."

"Not even to Shakespeare's?"

"Theatres are dens of iniquity. Forby, I've no time. It's all I can do to keep up with ma studies. I've . . . I've failed so often in my examinations I've had to take classes over again. I'm not clever, the way you always were."

"Aweel, your trials and tribulations should make you sympathetic to people, and that'll be useful in your chosen profession. Look, I'll give you the fare for the stagecoach. How much is it?"

"It's dear. Eight shillings for an outside seat and more if you want to be under cover. And you have to tip the driver and the porter and the guard. It could be twelve or thirteen bawbees, and there's the price of the food, if you can get any at the inns where they change horses."

Certainly not cheap, but by comparison with the money he had just deposited in the Royal Bank, the amount was infinitesimal. "I'll pay your fare, Alasdair, and for an inside seat. When's the morning departure?"

"I don't know, it's that long since I travelled that way. But there's a mail coach that leaves too, later on in the day."

"Then have more coffee, while I go and find some cash. And you must meet my wife and children," he added belatedly.

Upstairs, he found Jean and Clementina trying on bonnets and the two boys romping around with the young Sincerbeaux. His news sobered them, though Angus couldn't wait to see his uncle.

"He's studyin' for the ministry, is he no', Papa?"

"Aye, so come downstairs and he'll tell you how hard it is."

This last family reunion did not last long. Alasdair, tongue-tied from shyness when introduced to the Vicomtesse and Jean, seemed eager to leave, though his brother tried to get him to talk about his theological studies for Angus's benefit.

Douglas also insisted on giving him five pounds. Alasdair protested this was far too much but he accepted it nonetheless. Pocketing the money, he made to depart, in hopes, he claimed, of catching the stage coach which was more comfortable than the mail carrier.

As they parted at the front door he asked his brother, "Have you any messages for Father?"

Douglas hesitated. It might, he realised, be his last direct contact with the minister. "Tell him," he said finally, "that I'm sorry to hear about Mama. But, as a medical man, I am not surprised. And everything possible was done for her. I'll write to him, when I'm back in Strathblane." Mr Gardner would help him with the letter.

Then, conscious of a decision fast becoming irrevocable, he added, "You might also tell him – and Jenny, too – that an American physician, a Dutchman, has invited me to go into partnership with him in the city of New York. He is returning there shortly. He's been assisting an old professor of mine here, a position I once held myself. Before he leaves for the United States, I have to talk some more with him and decide whether or not I'll accept his offer."

"Oh, Dougie! Surely you wouldn't go to America! It's such a godless place and so far away!"

"Ach, come on, laddie! Nothing venture, nothing win."

PART V

STRATHBLANE AND AWAY

"God be with you till we meet again
By his counsel's guides uphold you.
With his sheep securely fold you
God be with you till we meet again."

Jeremiah E Rankin (1818–1904)
and set to a folk tune by
R Vaughn Williams in a hymnal
used in American Presbyterian churches.

I

For the remainder of that day and throughout the next, Clementina kept the sad Stewarts busy. She found black armbands for mourning and instead of going shopping she took Jean and the boys out in her little carriage to sightsee, leaving Douglas to himself.

Remembering how his mother had encouraged his love of music, he sat down at the piano, picking out chords and the notes of favourite melodies. Some day, in New York perhaps, he would buy an instrument like this and learn to play it properly.

When he was sufficiently calm, he wrote to Jock MacLean and warned him not to expect the family back in Strathblane immediately. Then he went out to see Peter van Buren. They discussed a partnership contract and called on a solicitor who agreed to draw one up for their signatures. The American also had suggestions on where to find information on emigration to the United States, and Douglas returned to Charlotte Square with a sizeable collection of papers to study.

Later in the day, he and Jean went with Clementina to visit Peter and Johanna at their modest flat in the Old Town, met their children and had more conversation, interspersed, from time to time, with music. The van Burens had decided against visiting Holland and were planning to return to New York within the month.

"So we'll be back home by the time you arrive, Doug,"

said Peter, "and rest assured, I'll be looking out for places you can stay and telling everyone what a great partner I'm getting!"

The pleasant evening did much to reinforce Douglas in his decision and seemed to reassure Jean, who had dutifully written to her cousin in Glasgow, telling him of their impending visit.

Willie MacDougal imported raw cotton which was woven into saleable cloth at the factory he owned in Strathblane. How he had ever had the imagination to create such a successful business was a mystery to Douglas who had never found any topic of conversation he could share with his wife's relative other than the Glasgow merchant's innumerable ailments for which he always sought advice, free of course, when they met.

On the long, slow journey to Glasgow, with the boys out of earshot sitting beside the coachman, the Stewarts talked over the projected American venture. And, without Clementina to dispel her fear, Jean's apprehension increased, possibly, her husband suspected, because of her queasy condition. But she seemed resigned to the inevitability of leaving the Blane Valley and when he told her of all that had happened in Edinburgh, she agreed that they should not try to move to the Capital or indeed, anywhere else in Scotland.

Fortunately, she had liked the van Burens, though what Johanna had told her about New York was disturbing. "I asked her, Dougie, if she didna mind living upstairs in yon wee Edinburgh land, and she said no, it was what she was used to in Manhattan. People there live gey close thegither. I've never done that. I've aye looked out on countryside and mountains."

"Peter says there are beautiful farms on Manhattan Island, and fine estates too."

"Aye, but the van Burens are well connected. I could tell that from the way she talked about their families. D'ye suppose we'd feel at home wi Dutch people?"

"There are a lot of Scots too. There's even a Presbyterian kirk to attend. And hospitals wi real interesting diseases from all over the world." Douglas could not hide his enthusiasm. "Jean, ye'll find plenty to interest you."

She sighed. "I suppose so. When Clemmie was showing off my embroidery the ither night, Johanna said I could make a business for masel in New York, sewing."

"Aye, and ye're guid at designing fashionable clothes, ma dearie, which would help us buy a nice house. Peter says he'll send me plenty of patients. And he told me I could give lectures, too, on animal magnetism at a college in the city. But we can stay in Scotland until ye've had this bairn. There's no rush for us to leave Strathblane."

What he heard in Glasgow, however, changed that. Over an enormously filling late afternoon dinner with the MacDougals, Jean had raised the subject of emigrating to America. Her cousin Willie had reacted as he always did, with a series of humphs and haws, while he shovelled quantities of meat and potatoes into his mouth. But his fat, sonsy wife had asked a number of knowledgable questions about their overseas prospects, as though well accustomed to doing so. And when the merchant was preparing to return to his place of business at the end of the meal, he said to Douglas, "Come and see me at the countin' house the morn. I hae ma lists o' sailings there. I've no much traffic wi New York but I do send ships up to the Hudson River ports, now and again."

"Where do you usually unload your cargoes?" the doctor asked.

"In the state of Virginia. There's an old established trade between Glasgow and the town of Alexandria. It started wi tobacco, in the last century, and now it's cotton."

"Could we disembark there? It might give us a chance to see a bit of the country."

"It's a fair distance. Ye'd have to board another ship to take ye up the coast and that might mean several more days at sea. And wi a' yer furniture, it could be expensive. I've books about the United States," he went on, to Douglas's surprise. "You can take a look at them. Come by at eight o'clock." He belched, "And if ye hae ony o' that new stomach medicine ye telt me about, bring me some of it."

Fair enough, thought the doctor. My expertise for yours. So, after he had taken his wife and children back to the inn to sleep off their dinner, he went in search of an apothecary, hoping a brisk walk would help digest his own meal.

II

Strolling along the banks of the Clyde, Dr Stewart looked down river and tried to imagine what it would be like to sail on one of the ships berthed there. As a student, he had been to Leith several times and gone aboard the huge grimy monsters picking up cargo there, but their constant movement, rising and falling in the harbour, and the overpowering smells from below decks, had invariably sent him back ashore quickly.

He was wondering how he could endure six weeks or more of life at sea, when a huge hand descended on his shoulder and a rough voice greeted him with, "Ahoy there, Surgeon Stewart!"

Turning, he looked into a familiar bearded face.

"Captain Abernethy!"

"And what brings ye to Glasgow, doctor?"

"A long story. And Willie Lamont too!" For a gangly young sailor was also extending a friendly paw with a thin white scar across its grimy back. Douglas ran his finger over it. "Never any problems wi that hand, eh, laddie?"

"Naw, sir. And I'm the first mate now."

"Congratulations."

"Hae ye time for a dram?" asked the Captain. "We're delivering some new brandy to yon pub across the road."

It might help his overloaded gut. "You know I never refuse." They headed into an ordinary where Douglas settled himself in a back booth while the Captain and Willie talked business. Abernethy then unabashedly demanded shot glasses and produced a bottle from his kitbag.

"Try some o' this, doctor. It's guid for whatever ails ye."

"It's the latest?"

"Aye. The French are livin' it up again, after a' the sober years o' the Revolution. How's Jean?"

"Breeding again."

"Eh, ye randy bastard. We made a delivery in Strathblane yesterday and I heard ye'd gone to Edinburgh."

Douglas told him the reason for the trip and Abernethy nodded sympathetically. He was a merchant seaman who, as well as legitimate cargo, carried contraband aboard his ship, the *Mary Ann*. Jean's father, who had stored this illegal merchandise in his Strathblane barn, had been killed during a raid by the Excise.

After their marriage, Douglas had forbidden his wife to involve herself in Strathblane's lucrative smuggling trade. Nevertheless, the doctor often treated sick or injured seamen in return for some untaxed brandy or French wine. He liked Abernethy and respected his knowledge of the world.

"Have you ever been to America, Captain?"

"Aye, several times, when they were fightin' their War of Independence. I mind we ran a blockage once, wi a lot of shooting."

"Where was that?"

"Down South off the Carolinas."

"Did you ever sail into New York?"

"Oh aye! Yon's a beautiful port."

Douglas sipped his brandy. "I met an American doctor in Edinburgh who came from what he called New Amsterdam. He's about to return there and he's offered me a partnership, if I'll join him. What would you do, if you were in my shoes, wi a wife and a growin' family?"

"Ye want to emigrate?"

"Aye. I've no future in Scotland, after that old trouble I had with the law."

Abernethy lit a malodorous pipe. "You could do a lot worse than settle in New York. The South's unco' hot most o' the year. Forby, the people are lazy, and there's a' that tradin' in slaves, which I think ye'd find uncongenial. But you'd like the Yankees. Was this man a Hollander?"

"Yes. His name's van Buren."

"A guid, solid family that owns a fair amount of property on Manhattan Island. He's probably far ben in the city so he could help you establish yourself. But if you're serious, doctor, you'd best go soon. Before we start the next war wi France. It'll be a long one unless we stop this Napoleon Bonaparte on land the way Lord Nelson's doing at sea."

"I heard rumours about more war in Edinburgh."

"It's more than rumours in Boulogne. I've a French wife, ye ken, and her relatives are aye talking politics. This Boney's just appointed hissel First Consul for life and the next thing, they say, he'll be named king or emperor, he's that ambitious. And these successful soldiers, they aye need to be winnin' victories to stay popular."

"I suppose the fighting could affect shipping?"

"Aye, indeed, and especially on the Atlantic. So if ye plan to go, sail as soon as ye can."

"Do you know anything about Willie MacDougal's ships?"

"Jean's cousin? Aye. His vessels are bigger than mine and sturdy, too. They're no luxurious but they only sink in real bad storms."

"I hear there are hurricanes in the Atlantic."

"Aye, but no until late August, usually. How far along is Jean's new bairn?"

"She shouldn't be brought to bed until after the end of the year."

"She'll take quite a batterin' aboard, if the seas are rough and they usually are, beyond the Clyde. Ach, but Jean's a strong lassie, and mony a captain's wife has given birth aboard a ship." He blew a reflective cloud of smoke from his pipe. "Willie MacDougal charges plenty for passage on his freighters. Tell him to sign ye on as ship's surgeon and gie yer wife and the bairns free transport."

"But I know nothing about maritime medicine!"

"Sailors suffer from the same ills as ither folk. They just hae more o' the clap and they break bones fallin' off the riggings. I'd make yin suggestion, Doctor. On a long voyage ye maun be sure they eat plenty o' fresh lemons and limes to guard against the scurvy."

"I'd heard about that. Anything else I should know?"

"No aff the top o' ma heid, but there's a couple of old Navy doctors here in Glasgow that I keep supplied wi duty free rum. D'ye want to pick their brains?"

"Yes. How long will you be in port?"

"Most o' the week. I've still cargo to unload down in

Greenock, and I'll be back up here in the town looking for freight for my return voyage so I can tak' ye with me and introduce ye to some useful people."

"Then we'll meet again, and after I've talked to Willie the morn. This brandy is beautiful! I'd like some of it for Mr Paterson. He made my trip possible, lending us his carriage and coachman."

"I'll leave a couple of bottles for ye at the Inn. One is for yersel."

Douglas dug into his pocket. "So how much do I owe you?"

"Doctor, you and I have never charged one another for services and we're no startin' the now."

III

Next morning, the two little boys accompanied Rabb and Hannibal to the veterinarian's, and Jean, carrying Meg, went with Douglas to Willie MacDougal's counting house. The doctor was well armed with stomach medicines.

"These pills should put him in a guid frame of mind," he told Jean. "I'll suggest he take one as soon as we arrive."

"Aye. Then let me do the talking, Dougie, and especially the bargaining. He's my kinsman, after all."

"And you are much better at business than I am, dear wife."

In his office, the merchant showed more signs of intelligence than he did in private life, with a firm grip on facts and figures. He was studying a big ledger when they entered his office.

"I've gey few sailings to the Hudson River ports," he told them, without preamble. "As I telt ye yesterday, most o' ma trade is wi Alexandria and that's too far South for ye. The only vessel on the Northern run this summer leaves Port Glasgow around the end of July. And that'll be the last trip to New York until next Spring."

"It doesna gie us much time to make arrangements," said Jean.

"Ye'd hae a guid six weeks to pack."

"Yes and all the documents. . ." said the doctor.

"I can help ye wi those. I ken who to bribe, if there's ony problem. I've a man here who can handle that kind o' detail for I usually take a few passengers on every voyage. So dinna fash yersel. Just be packed and ready to embark at short notice, when the ship docks in Port Glasgow."

"Could we see over it ahead of time?" Douglas asked. "So Jean would know what our accommodations would be like?"

Willie shook his head. "That vessel's on the high seas the now. But ye can go aboard ma other ships, if ye want to gang doon the wa'er. They're a' built much the same."

"I think we should do that."

But Jean, her face pale, refused. "Naw. If we're leavin' so soon, we maun go straight to Strathblane." Later, back at the inn, she confessed, "I was feared I'd lose ma courage. If we're goin', we're goin' and it makes no difference how uncomfortable the voyage may be."

"Could ye pack everything up by the end of July?"

"Oh aye. We've no that much and what we dinna take we can leave in the house for Jock and Mamie. I suppose they'll be movin' in there?"

"Aye, and they'll take on Mrs MacGregor unless she decides to retire. The wee cottage they're in is too small for them wi their family growing. Besides, Blaerisk is part of the practice and I'd aye promised it to him, once he was qualified. I'll leave him my collection of medical specimens and some of my books too."

"Johanna telt me they make guid furniture in New York, so I'll just take a few heirlooms – like the sideboard and the clock and the fourposter bed."

He quoted reflectively,

There is a tide in the affairs of men that taken
at the flood leads on to fortune.

Odd that Willie had been thinking about taking on a ship's surgeon. . ."

"Aye. It's strange, is it no', Dougie? – the way things are starting to happen to us. As if they'd been foreordained. First Walter's wife died, and then yer mother, and then we got a' that money. And what happened in Edinburgh. And now Willie havin' that one ship going to New York. . ." But she couldn't hold back her tears. "So soon. . ."

He invoked his favourite Shakespeare play, *"If it were done when 'tis done, then 'twere well 'twere done quickly."*

"Aye, but this isna surgery. It's our whole future, ours and our children's."

"I know. And, my dearie, I do know how much of a sacrifice it is to you to leave your home. But I can't be a country doctor all my life."

"I've kennt that from the first day we ever met, Dougie."

IV

In the mysterious way of the country, news of the Stewarts' impending departure from the Blane Valley arrived in Strathblane before them and Walter Paterson was on the doorstep of Blaerisk as Hannibal and the other horse were returning to their stable.

"So now you're off to America," said the laird of Leddrie Green.

Jean burst into tears. Her husband just nodded. Before they could say more, the little boys came running in.

"Mr Paterson, when can I come over and see Anne?" Tommy demanded. "I brought her a book from Edinburgh called *The Life and* . . ." his brow wrinkled, *"Per-am-bulations of a Mouse."*

"That sounds like an interesting story."

"Aye, and it has nice pictures, too."

"Well, you can bring it over any time. Why don't you come tomorrow after school? Maybe your Papa can come too and take a look at her at the same time."

"What's the matter?" asked Tommy, one second ahead of the doctor.

"Probably nothing. But . . . she and Mary don't seem as lively as usual and I want to be sure they're quite well." He added, "I suppose you've heard that my mother was here on a visit? She just went back to Edinburgh. She brought my cousin Betsy with her and she has stayed on to run my household."

"Aye, Clementina telt us," said Jean. "Is she bein' a help to ye?"

"I suppose so. I did need someone to order the meals and see that the girls did their lessons." He sounded unenthusiastic. "You'll have to meet her, Jean." He didn't say when.

The following afternoon, Douglas picked up his second son at the school house and they rode over to Leddrie Green, both of them perched on old Maggie, for Dr Jock MacLean had already pre-empted the practice's younger horse. Betsy Paterson and the doctor took an immediate dislike to each other. She was a tall woman past her first youth, with strong features and thick eyebrows that matched her dark hair, completely different in appearance and personality from Walter's dead wife.

"She's a snob," Douglas complained later to Jean. "She treated me like a lackey. And she watched my every move as if she thought I'd try to ravish the two wee girls."

Mary and Anne Paterson had known him all their lives. He had brought both of them into the world and they had never been afraid of him. But with their aunt hovering stiffly in the background they had been tense and uncommunicative with none of the usual laughter at the little jokes he made to distract them during his examinations.

He could find nothing wrong, physically, and to get them away from her, he suggested they go with him to the stables where Walter had taken Tommy for a reunion with Rabb and Hannibal.

"Be careful you don't get dirty, girls," Betsy admonished them. "And, remember! No riding, not even around the yard in those dresses!"

Tommy ran to greet his little friend Anne who was delighted with what she immediately christened, 'the Mousy book.' Jean had sent a little gift to Mary too.

"And I've something for you, Paterson," Douglas patted his bag. "Can we leave our children here with Rabb and go indoors?"

"Come along."

In Walter's library, the doctor produced the brandy. "I saw Captain Abernethy in Glasgow. This is the latest from France, and very smooth it is."

"Thank you. Shall we sample it now?"

"No. It's for you to take at bedtime. When you've finished your literary labours for the night."

Walter sighed. "My writing is not going well."

"Nor do you look well, my friend. You're much too thin and for a man who spends so much time outdoors, you're unco' pale. Not having seen you for several weeks, I notice a change in you and it's not a healthy one. Since

I'm here, maybe I should examine you too."

"No. I'm thin because I have no appetite. I can't eat all this rich food Betsy serves up. She says it's fashionable. And I miss Primrose more and more. I don't sleep well without her. . ." He sighed. "I'm tired all the time."

"Aye, sadness makes you tired as I'm finding out myself."

Walter put out a sympathetic hand. "Yes. You've lost your mother. And your old mentor too. And now you're getting ready to leave us, I can't believe it. . ."

"It had to come some time, Paterson. And there's that much to be done before we go, it's taking my mind off my griefs." Douglas took a long breath. "I couldn't say this to you before, it was too soon, but . . . as a physician, I've seen much of bereavement, and believe me, it's true that time heals. But you need patience, which you, my friend, have never had. It was your biggest problem, when you were recovering from those wounds you suffered in France."

"Yes. I remember. But those were physical difficulties, not emotional ones. Except of course, that I'd just fallen in love with Primrose and I couldn't wait to marry her." Walter shrugged with a mannerism left over from his French upbringing. "*C'est la vie.* . . Never mind about my health. What about my daughters?"

"Set your mind at rest. There's no consumption. But they are grieving just as you are and they're less able to understand it. They need your help, Paterson, and you need theirs."

"What should I do, Stewart?"

"Spend as much time with them as you can. Mamie MacLean tells me the baby's flourishing. She complains he's draining her of so much milk she can scarce keep her own bairn fed."

Walter nodded without enthusiasm. "Yes. At least my heir seems to be doing well."

Trying to keep up the conversation, the doctor went on. "Angus came back from Darnick determined to be a minister. But my second son claims he wants to go into medicine. So I telt him on the way over here that now was the time to start learning to diagnose. Children confide in each other more freely than they do in us adults, so maybe he'll have learned what is bothering your daughters."

Walter smiled for the first time. "Let me know what he says. He's a remarkably mature child. On our way to the stables, we had quite a conversation."

"Did he tell you he planned to be a surgeon, so he could afford to marry Anne?"

"Well! Well!" Walter laughed, as Douglas had hoped he would. "Now tell me about Edinburgh. And what news did my sister have from France?"

The two old friends were deep in a discussion of how the serious international situation might affect the Stewarts' emigration plans when Betsy walked in, carrying a dainty tray.

"It's teatime, Walter." As if it was an afterthought she asked, "Should I fetch a cup for Doctor Stewart?"

Douglas stood up. "No thank you, Miss Paterson. I must be on my way. Where's Tommy? Still in the stables with Anne?"

She looked mildly shocked. "No. I brought the girls in. Your little boy is waiting in the hall and Rabb has your horse ready for you."

Walter, a little embarrassed at this curt termination of the visit, walked to the front door and lifted Tommy up into his father's arms when the doctor had mounted, saying quietly, "Let us meet again soon, *mon brave*, and have more talk."

As they rode across the valley, Douglas asked, "Well, Doctor Stewart-the-Younger, what's your diagnosis? Why are Anne and Mary so peekit?"

The little boy chewed on his thumb then said, "They dinna like their new auntie."

"Why not?"

"She's awful particular. They maun be quiet in the house, and she doesna like them goin' outside for fear they get dirty. But she'll no let them tak' the new puppies up to the schoolroom to play. Awful nice wee beasties they are too. Is this what ye need to ken, Papa?"

"Aye. Go on, laddie, you're doing fine. What else?"

"She's that scared o' horses, they never go out on their ponies. And she makes them eat everything on their plates, even when it's spinach."

"You can sympathize with that."

"Aye. And nae sweeties because they're bad for their teeth."

"They are too, but now and again they'll no hurt."

"Can I take Anne some sweeties, Papa?"

"Ye maun ask Mr Paterson for permission first."

And how, he wondered, could he tell his friend what his daughters had said about Betsy?

Jean advised, "Gie him the truth. I've a feelin' Walter's no that fond of her hissel."

"Then why doesn't he send her packing?"

"It's no that easy, Dougie. She's his cousin and his mother brought her here to run the household. Who's to do it, if she goes?"

"Can't it run itself?"

"Oh no! There's orderin' the meals, making jam, putting up meat and fruit to preserve for the winter. And a' the sewing and mending. It's a fair responsibility an establishment like Leddrie Green. And Walter's got his hands full wi his planting. He hasna the time to keep an eye on the cook and the maids."

"Aye, and he's that low, if yon woman tries to marry him, he'll no have the strength to refuse her."

"That's what I'm afraid of, Dougie. Wi a' his family in Edinburgh hoping for a match, how can he resist?"

V

At Kirklands House, Mrs Henry Moncrieff was also worrying about Walter Paterson. She was the most influential woman in Strathblane, not simply as the Laird's wife but because of her intelligent concern for the well being of her friends and neighbours. Even the village people listened to her practical advice.

Pleasant and comfortable in appearance, Alison in her youth had been married to a Glasgow financier, Robert Graham, who had been older than she was. When he died, leaving her with a sickly child also named Robert, she had moved to Strathblane, to Leddrie Green House. Walter Paterson bought the property from her when she took Henry Moncrieff for her second husband.

Bobby Graham had grown up to be an unremarkable but amiable young man who shared his mother's fondness for resolving other people's problems. He had left home to go into business in Glasgow but on his visits to Strathblane, he always made a point of seeing Walter who had once been his tutor and was more like a parent to him than his stepfather.

When Walter's mother and Betsy arrived in the valley, Alison Moncrieff had entertained them to tea at Kirklands House and the impression this meeting left behind disturbed her. So, when her eldest son next visited

Strathblane, she took the opportunity to invite the widower and his cousin to supper.

"Now, Bobby" she had said, before they arrived, "I want your candid opinion of the girl. Your Uncle Walter simply must marry again and soon, for his own sake as much as the children's. Obviously his family thinks Betsy would be a suitable bride for him."

"But you don't, Mama?"

"I'm not sure. I've only met her once and she didn't say much, with Mrs Paterson there. And I couldn't imagine how she might strike a man. It's no use asking Henry, he doesn't notice women."

"He noticed you!"

"That was different. He was looking for a wife in those days. Bobby, I'm curious to know if you think your Uncle Walter and this cousin of his are congenial."

"Dr Stewart's always been the local authority in those matters, Mama. What does he say about her?"

Alison threw up her hands. "He doesn't say anything, which is ominous! When he came up with some new pills for Henry, I tried to draw him out on the subject of Betsy and all I could gather was that they weren't exactly drawn to each other. But the doctor's a bit prickly. Sometimes he sees slights when they aren't meant."

"Well, I'll look the lady over and tell you, from the masculine viewpoint, if she's suitable."

"Oh Bobby! I'd be so grateful! And now tell me, when are you going to pick out a nice bride for yourself?"

"Mama! Don't start that again! I'm having much too good a time flirting with the pretty girls in Glasgow!"

The supper party was not a success. Walter arrived looking withdrawn and apathetic, though he was glad to see Bobby. Betsy, in Edinburgh finery, was overdressed for the country and when they went out to admire the new rock garden, she put more effort into keeping her skirts and slippers clean than into admiring the flowers. Handsome rather than pretty, she nevertheless affected feminine mannerisms like constantly flirting her fan, a superfluous accessory in the cool evening.

Over sherry, the chief topic of conversation was the Stewart family's projected move to America. The Laird, a dedicated hypochondriac, was against it since he believed, with truth, that the doctor understood his innumerable ailments. Henry Moncrieff had found Doctor Jock MacLean a competent phlebotomist, but he could never forget that the young man had been a footman at Kirklands House before he became Douglas Stewart's apprentice. The Laird also disapproved of the United States. He thought the Americans should have remained colonists and could not imagine why any intelligent person would want to live in an undeveloped country surrounded by savage Indians.

Walter, when Alison asked his opinion, said simply that he understood the doctor's desire to move, and added he would miss him sorely. Betsy was silent, her eyes roving over the good looking Bobby Graham.

At table the talk turned, as it usually did between the Laird and his brother-in-law, on the state of their respective crops. Betsy seemed no more interested in these than in flowers. Bobby, to bring her into the conversation, steered it towards politics and the prospects of war. On these topics she proved extremely vocal. Henry Moncrieff did not care for opinionated women. He turned silent and so did Walter.

As soon as she decently could, Alison Moncrieff rose from the supper table and took the other lady off to the drawing room, leaving the gentlemen to their port. However her son made sure they did not sit over it long and when they joined the ladies, Alison invited Betsy to play the piano. She was not as pleasing a performer as Primrose had been, so Bobby, at a signal from his mother, suggested a rubber of whist.

The Laird did not play. He settled himself down at the far end of the room to read a farming publication. Walter usually enjoyed a good game of cards, but that evening he was inattentive and when his turn came to be dummy, he drifted away from the table and resumed the discussion about agriculture with his host. After the game ended – in a clear victory for Bobby and Betsy as partners – Walter said he must leave because he had to be up early to supervise some estate work.

"And I fear I'm not very sociable these days," he confessed. "But Bob, please come over tomorrow morning and have some coffee with me. I'm anxious to hear more about what you're doing in Glasgow."

On his return from this visit, the young man went straight to his mother's parlour.

"Well?" she asked, once she had chased away her two small children who adored their big stepbrother and wanted to monopolize him. "What about it, Bobby?"

He shook his head. "It's worse than you suspected. She's all wrong for him and he doesn't know how to fend her off."

"Did he tell you that?"

"No. He didn't have to. The stupid woman wouldn't let us enjoy our chat in peace. She had to butt in and pour coffee for us. Finally, I made some excuse about wanting to see a newly planted field and we were able to escape outdoors. What bothered me was that Uncle Walter didn't seem able to get away from her. Either he didn't have the energy or he didn't know how."

Alison sighed. "I gather that's what happened with Dr Stewart, too. I think she means well. She was trying to be a good hostess."

"But she has no sense, Mama. You wouldn't have stayed around. You would have brought in the refreshment and then made some excuse to leave us alone. Now wouldn't you?"

"Probably. Oh dear!"

"And she has it in mind to marry him. When you're a single man you recognize the signs. Smiles and possessive pats on the shoulder. Little jokes that other people don't understand. That sort of thing. And she was trying to flirt with me last night, to make him jealous. But you're right. He's terribly lonely. And, I suspect he's frustrated." Bobby looked carefully away and added "Physically, I mean. That's probably why he can't sleep."

She nodded. Then asked, "Would it help him if you took him to Glasgow to meet . . . some women?"

Her son was shocked. "You mean whores? No! Look, when he was my tutor, I was at an age to be curious and we talked about things I could only ask a man. He was frank with me about . . . well, his own youthful peccadillos and he told me it was warmth and affection that attracted him to women, not beauty and well . . . Besides," he added bluntly, "that Betsy's getting on and she looks like a cold fish. But she needs a husband badly, and he's available."

"Then what are we going to do, Bobby?"

He paced up and down the parlour. "We have to find a woman he might like and move her into his house, somehow. Maybe to copy his manuscripts or as a governess for the girls."

"Yes, I'd thought of that too. But there's no-one in the valley. . ."

"What about my cousin-once-removed, Christina Graham? Kirsty as we've always called her. Last year you suddenly wanted *me* to marry her. I could never think why."

"Oh, Bobby, her father had just died and her mother

was worrying that she'd never find a husband because she had no dowry."

"So you spoke up and said, *How about my son who's already well provided for?*"

"Yes, and I never did understand why nothing came of it. You'd always liked her."

"But we grew up like brother and sister. And nowadays, with all this talk about freedom and everyone reading romantic poetry, people of our generation want to marry for love."

"Unions can be successful when they're based on affection and mutual respect." She was thinking of her own with Henry Moncrieff.

"That's not how Kirsty feels and I agree with her. But she's a nice girl and she could be very pretty if she had some decent clothes. Well educated too. After all, she's a minister's daughter."

"Yes, she'd be ideal in Walter's household. I'll write to her today and invite her here for a little visit."

"Tell her she'd better come soon," Bobby advised. "That Betsy could move in for the kill any time."

Kirsty Graham arrived within the week. Though she lived near Tarbet on Loch Lomondside, she had seldom visited Strathblane, and then only briefly for she had nursed her father through a long illness. While her widowed mother was recuperating at Kirklands, Alison, who found her cousin-by-marriage a rather ineffectual woman, had tried to impress upon her that her daughter should have some career to support her if she was unlikely to marry. So now the Laird's wife wrote a letter, saying she knew of a suitable opportunity for employment in the Blane valley and enclosing money for the journey.

Henry Moncrieff scarcely noticed Kirsty, but when he did, he approved of her and remarked to his wife that the way she played the piano reminded him of his dead sister, Primrose. This, Alison thought, was a good omen.

The next problem was how to insinuate her into the Leddrie Green household and here Betsy, inadvertently, played into Mrs Moncrieff's hand with an invitation to tea at Leddrie Green. Alison went by herself.

"Oh, but you should have brought your cousin with you!" exclaimed her hostess. "It would have been no trouble to set out an extra cup and I would so like to meet her."

"Christina is very shy," said the Laird's wife. "She hasn't been out much in society, and her father's death left the family in straightened circumstances." She sighed. "The poor girl is here looking for work. Do you know of any family that needs a governess? She's good with children."

Betsy threw up her hands, laughed prettily and exclaimed, "That's a gift I don't have! I have no success in disciplining my nieces."

"Oh, Miss Paterson! They're exceptionally well behaved little girls!"

"Only when they feel like it. And the children they associate with at the village school are so uncouth. The way they speak! Mary and Anne will need a great deal of polishing before they go to Edinburgh and come out in society."

"Does their father want them to do that?"

"I don't imagine he's thought much about it. After all, they're only eight and six years' old."

"But one must look ahead," Alison agreed and switched the conversation to other matters.

Betsy considered herself intellectual and she liked to discuss the books she read. If only, she sighed, Walter would consult her about the manuscript he was striving to complete. . .

"Have you suggested copying it out?" asked Alison.

"That is such a tedious job. Primrose used to do it for him."

"I've never been a copyist, I've always edited. But I suppose. . ." Betsy sighed. "I find I have enough to do here just trying to train the servants to prepare the food properly."

The Laird's wife feared the worst. Good cooks were hard to find in the country and the excellent one at Leddrie Green was well known to dislike interference in her kitchen. However, before Alison could ask more questions, Walter drifted into the drawing room and his apathetic face lit up at the sight of her. "Betsy, why didn't you tell me my sister-in-law was coming to tea?"

She wrinkled her long nose at him in a manner she clearly thought was appealing. "We wanted to have some woman-talk, my dear."

"Well, d'you mind if I join you for a cup?"

"Of course not. In fact, there's something I want to talk to you about, Walter. Mrs Moncrieff has a cousin staying with her who's looking for a situation as a governess. She would be suitable for Mary and Anne."

"What do they need a governess for? They're getting excellent instruction at the parish school."

"Oh, but Walter, they're not learning the manners of polite society! The village children are so common!"

"Primrose planned to send them to a young ladies' boarding school when it came time to acquire the fashionable graces."

"Wouldn't you rather keep them at home, Walter?" interposed Alison.

"For a few years, yes, of course."

"Then perhaps we should take on Miss Graham," pursued Betsy. "Suitable governesses are very hard to find. She's available and we know who she is."

He sighed, as though to make such a decision was beyond him. "I'm not sure if I can afford another salary at present."

"She wouldn't be expensive," Alison put in. "It would be her first situation so she'd be working for the experience, as you did with Bobby. I didn't pay *you* very much, as you may remember."

He smiled. "It seemed a lot of money to me at the time. But I'm not sure it would be a good idea to introduce changes into the girls' lives at present. To take them out of school, away from all their little friends in Strathblane, could add to the loneliness they feel. With no mother, I mean," he explained.

Betsy went on, "They could stay in school. Miss Graham would be teaching them things like art and embroidery and the pianoforte. She'd keep them busy in the afternoons and be company for them, which would free you for your literary work."

"Dr Stewart told me I should spend time with my daughters. And Primrose always helped them with their schoolwork."

"But it takes you away from your writing and your publisher is anxiously waiting for your next book."

"Let that be, please, Betsy. It's a different matter and one I can't do anything about, I fear."

"But this is such a good opportunity to get the right person. Mrs Moncrieff, why don't you let us meet her? That wouldn't commit you in any way, Walter."

"No, but . . . Oh very well." He poured himself tea, which Betsy hadn't done. "Bring the woman over here at this time tomorrow, if you will, Alison."

VI

Kirsty Graham, either because she was scared or, more likely, because she had not made up her own mind about her future, was unusually quiet when she accompanied Alison to Leddrie Green. She also failed to do justice to her good looks, putting on a dark cotton dress and a drab bonnet that hid her pretty hair. She stubbornly refused offers of shawls and ribbons to spruce up her appearance.

Betsy was overpoweringly gracious, which increased Kirsty's apparent shyness. Walter asked her where she came from, made some remarks about Loch Lomond and the scenery around Tarbet, then he fell silent.

His cousin however, cross-questioned the young woman on her family, her education, the books she read and, in particular, her experience in taking care of children.

"I have four little sisters, Miss Paterson. They go to the village school for Latin and mathematics, but I've been teaching them to dance and to talk French."

"*Vous parlais francais?*" asked Walter, with a flicker of interest. He had grown up in Paris.

"*Oui, monsieur. Un peu. Et j'aime beaucoup . . .*"

"I read French fluently," Betsy interrupted. "But I haven't had much practice in speaking it. How did you learn that, Miss Graham?"

"My father used it in conversation with us at home. He had made a grand tour of Europe as a young man. Before my grandfather lost his money in a disastrous overseas investment."

"I talk to my daughters in French too whenever I can," said Walter "I want them to grow up bilingual, as I did."

Betsy, striking when the iron seemed hot, said, "Good. Then Miss Graham would be just right to tutor them."

But she was moving too fast. "No," said Walter. "I don't want anyone else in the house at present. I'm sorry, Miss Graham. I don't mean to be offensive. Or evasive either. But I have to think more about the kind of person my daughters should have as a governess and that's in the future anyway."

"Walter, they're the proper age now! They . . ."

"Yes, yes, I know, but I'm not sure the timing is right or even the individual, in the circumstances. . ." His eyes flicked quickly over Kirsty, who now surprised Alison by speaking up.

"I agree with you, Mr Paterson. We need to be better acquainted. But in the meantime and regardless of what you may decide, I would like to meet your daughters."

"If you wish. Where are they, Betsy?"

"Upstairs in their schoolroom." She rang a little handbell and a maid materialised. "Bring the children down here, Annie. Then while we're waiting for the girls, Walter can show you his flowers." She led the way to the garden, and they were admiring his latest roses when Mary and Anne appeared.

Betsy immediately criticised them. "Girls, you should wear your pretty new dresses when you come down to meet visitors! And your hair! Didn't Annie brush it?"

"No, because you said we were to hurry!" Mary protested.

"Sorry, Aunt Betsy," said Anne, as they bobbed curtsies.

Kirsty stretched out welcoming arms. "I'm Christina Graham. Which of you is Mary and which is Anne?" They giggled and identified themselves. "You are both very pretty," she told them. "And your Papa says you have your own little garden that you plant and weed and water." They nodded, jumping up and down, eager to make friends.

"Yes," said Walter. "Show Miss Graham your flowerbeds, girls."

Taking Kirsty by the hand, one on each side, they guided her through the rockery. But she was still within earshot when their father remarked, "She's far too young to be their governess."

"She's young but she's capable, Walter," whispered Alison, a finger on her lip. When the children had gone, she told him, "Christina managed her little brothers and sisters at Tarbet so well after their father died that her mother was able to leave them and come to Strathblane for a holiday. And that was six months ago. I remember because you brought Primrose over to see her and it was one of the last times she was at Kirklands."

He nodded grimly. Betsy laid a firm hand on his arm. "Now, Walter, you mustn't dwell on the past. Think of your daughters' future."

"I still don't believe I want Miss Graham here." He strode off in the direction of the stables and did not return. When the visitors left Betsy said, with an attempt at lightness, that it was very ill-mannered of him not to come and say goodbye.

In the carriage going back to Kirklands, Kirsty started to cry. "He doesn't want me!" she sobbed. "He thinks I'm just a child!"

"My dear girl, don't be distressed. I'll find you a position in another household."

"But I don't want to be in another household! I want to be in that one!" She was angry as well as upset. "And he might have wanted me, too, if Miss Paterson hadn't tried to push him. She wouldn't let the poor man make up his own mind."

True indeed, thought Alison.

"He's so full of sadness," Kirsty went on. "So confused

and angry. He's the way I was after I lost Papa. Poor Mr Paterson. . . Such a fine figure of a man, and with such beautiful, intelligent blue eyes and that nice fair hair! Those essays of his about country life are so clever, I was starting to ask him about them, and in French, when that cousin interrupted me and she talked so much, she never gave me another chance. . . "

"Have you read Walter's essays?"

"Oh yes. And his poetry too. I found copies in Cousin Henry's library, and took them up to bed with me last night."

Alison gave her a sharp look. "Perhaps you should stay on here for a few days. I'll ask him over to dinner and make sure you have a chance to talk to him about his books."

"You'd have to invite Miss Paterson too," Kirsty pointed out, sniffing. "And please, Cousin Alison! I couldn't bear to see him again. I want to go home. Please! Let me leave tomorrow on the afternoon coach!"

She refused to be talked out of this decision. By noon next day she had packed up her few possessions, and was in the process of transporting them downstairs preparatory to departure when Walter turned up at Kirklands, alone and on horseback. The brisk ride had put colour in his cheeks, adding to his handsomeness, but he looked harassed and tense.

"Alison, please forgive my turning up like this uninvited, but we've a crisis at Leddrie Green."

"Don't apologise, Walter dear. Just come in and tell us what's happened."

"Betsy's mother has had an accident. She fell and broke her hip. There was a letter, in today's post. Betsy's so distressed, I told her she must go back home to Edinburgh at once."

He turned towards Kirsty who was standing in the hall, a small valise in one hand and her bonnet in the other." Miss Graham, could you come over and take charge while she's away?"

Allison was starting to say this was a wonderful idea when her young relative interrupted.

"No. I'm sorry, Mr Paterson. I'm going home to Tarbet today."

His face fell. "Oh. I didn't realise. You didn't say yesterday that you were leaving so soon. I understood you were here to look for a position."

"I am, Mr Paterson, but as a governess. Not as a temporary housekeeper."

Surprised, he bowed and said, "I beg your pardon, *mademoiselle*. I did not mean to downplay your abilities. But you *are* looking for a place and I need someone to run my establishment. Now. And possibly only for a short time. I would do my best to make it pleasant for you and compensate you well for your trouble."

"Money," said Kirsty tightly, "is not the point."

She set her bonnet on her shining hair. "I would be in an impossible position with your servants, Mr Paterson. They would not heed me, knowing my authority over them was only for the moment. Besides," her clear voice gained confidence, "my talents are for bringing up children rather than for housewifery. Although, like everyone else in the country, I know how to make preserves and salt meat. And yesterday, when I said I was seeking a position, it was a permanent one. I expected to be hired with the under-standing that, should I prove satisfactory, I would stay until your daughters were sent away to boarding school."

"Yes," he said. "That's the usual arrangement with governesses."

"But you thought I was too young. I heard you say

that. So, until I am older, I am going back to my own family, who also need me." She drew on a shabby pair of white crocheted gloves. "They like and respect me, too."

"Miss Graham, my children liked and respected you yesterday."

"But *you* didn't, Mr Paterson." Her eyes met his with a gentle boldness. "I won't work for people who doubt my abilities and . . . and who may need me at the moment but . . . don't really want me in their home."

Walter stared. "Whatever made you think I didn't want you?"

"You said so yesterday, Mr Paterson."

Now she had his full attention. "I didn't know whether or not I wanted the girls to have a governess. It was a new idea for me. There was nothing personal. . . I am sorry, Miss Graham. Evidently I didn't express myself properly. Or even courteously. I am not always myself these days. I sincerely beg your pardon."

She lowered her eyes. "Thank you, sir. I accept your apology."

"Then . . . will you come to Leddrie Green?"

She shook her head. "I have told you why I will not."

Alison started to make a suggestion, then, seeing the look on Kirsty's face, she held her peace. Besides, Walter had now assessed the situation or thought he had. "If I were to offer you a permanent position – as a governess – would you reconsider, Miss Graham?"

She said nothing.

"Please!" His voice warmed. "I need you. And my daughters need you too. Both for instruction and care. And do not worry about your position in the household. I would make it plain to my servants that you were in full charge. My cousin Betsy," he went on, "may well not come back from Edinburgh. I told her that her duty was to her own family, not to mine. And I suspect," he added, "that she doesn't really like living in the country."

Kirsty stayed silent but now she was attentive.

He continued, "Mary and Anne have been terribly lost without their mother. Their health has not been affected as yet, but it could be. And mine too, the doctor tells me."

"Yes, those poor children . . . For their sake, perhaps I should change my plans."

"And since you are already packed," Alison pointed out, "you could move over to Leddrie Green at once."

"Yes. I could go with you now, Mr Paterson."

His face brightened. He bowed, reached courteously for her gloved hand and kissed it. Then the worry came back into his eyes. "But I cannot offer you my carriage today. Rabb, my coachman, is up the valley bringing back a new horse for Betsy's trip to Edinburgh."

"We do have carriages here at Kirklands," said Alison.

"Yes. I know you do." He turned back to Kirsty. "My cousin isn't leaving for a couple of days. She says she must organize the household, plan menus. . .That of course will make it easier for you, Miss Graham."

"I'll bring her over tomorrow afternoon," said the Laird's wife, taking charge. "So now you don't need your bonnet, Kirsty. And Walter, you have time for a glass of sherry before you go."

Over the midday meal at Leddrie Green, he said to Betsy, "If I can complete some chapters on my book before you go, would you take them to my publishers in Edinburgh?"

"Why, of course, Walter."

"There's a lot to do but I can certainly get something together."

"Why don't I help you with the manuscript's preparation? What needs to be done?"

"Well, it must be copied out in a clear hand with my insertions and revisions worked into the text."

"I could start on it this afternoon."

"Don't you have a lot of packing?"

"Oh no. I'm not taking much luggage, I've plenty of dresses in Edinburgh."

"Betsy, you may be there some time. You must stay with your mother as long as she needs you. She's seriously incapacitated and as I well know, broken bones take a long time to heal, especially in an elderly person."

"Oh, she won't need me, once she's able to get up and move about. I'll try not to leave you alone for too long."

"I don't want you to feel any obligation to me and mine. . ."

She smiled coyly at him. "But I do, Walter. You are so sweet. So considerate. Now don't worry about me. Go and fetch your manuscript."

"Yes, I'd better be sure you can read my handwriting."

"Of course, I can! I've seen lots of it, in your letters." She was implying an intimacy he couldn't understand, for he did not recall ever corresponding with her, though he'd occasionally sent her messages in notes to his mother or sister. But he was thankful he could send his editor some tangible evidence that he was working on his book, set aside after his wife's death. Transcribing it was so tedious, he had kept putting it off.

Alison brought Kirsty over next day, and Walter was present to make her welcome. The little girls came in and when he told them Miss Graham was going to take care of them while their 'aunt' was in Edinburgh, they looked pleased.

As they took her off to show her their schoolroom, Betsy said, "Annie will unpack your valise, Miss Graham. You will have the bedroom next to the nursery."

"It's small but it's only for one night," Walter added quickly. "Tomorrow you can move downstairs to Miss Paterson's room."

"Oh." Betsy looked a little put out. "Then I'd have to put my clothes away. I hadn't planned. . . There's still a lot to do on your manuscript and I haven't much time. . ."

Kirsty turned and said quietly, "I don't need a big room, thank you, Mr Paterson."

That evening, she did not appear at the supper table, which, as usual, was set for two.

"Isn't Miss Graham joining us?" Walter asked.

Betsy shook her head. "She'll take her evening meal with the children. Governesses always do that."

"This governess is Alison Moncrieff's kinswoman. I think she should sup with us."

"Well, she can, from now on. But this is our last evening together, Walter. We should be alone."

He didn't see why, but he could change the domestic arrangements after Betsy had gone, so he ignored this remark and asked, "How are you progressing with my manuscript?"

She beamed. "I've completed it! I'll give it to you after we've finished our meal."

He was picking at his food, which he found heavy and potentially indigestible. Betsy also was eating little.

"I'm afraid," she remarked," that Hannah doesn't understand the preparation of sauces."

"No. Neither Primrose nor I liked them. They're too rich."

"Not if they're correctly made, Walter dear. I've tried to tell Hannah but . . ." she sighed and shrugged her shoulders.

"Well, it doesn't matter, Betsy. I've little appetite these days."

Usually in the evenings they sat in the drawing room, drank a demitasse of coffee and talked or at least Betsy did. Then Walter would go to his library, ostensibly to write, and she would read or otherwise entertain herself until they had a nightcap of cocoa and retired to their respective beds. But now he was heading upstairs.

"Where are you going?" she asked.

"I want to be sure that Miss Graham is comfortably settled and let her know she's to eat in the dining room from here on."

"I'll tell her tomorrow, Walter, before I go."

"Betsy, I feel I should apologise to her."

The childrens' quarters were on the top floor. The nursery was empty since the baby was still with Doctor MacLean's wife, Mamie who was acting as wet nurse. The two little girls shared a big airy bedroom with a dressing room next door. Scarcely large enough to hold a bed and a chest of drawers, it was used only when a child was sick and the nursemaid needed to be close by. This was where Betsy had installed the new governess.

Walter knocked on the door and, after a minute, a scared little voice asked, "Who is there, please?"

"Mr Paterson."

"Oh!"

"May I have a word with you, please? Unless you've gone to bed."

"No." The door opened. "Please come in."

The counterpane was turned down and she had thrown a big dark plaid over her plain white nightgown. In her arms she cradled his late wife's favourite cat.

"So this is where Blackie's been hiding," remarked Walter, stroking its head. "I missed him downstairs tonight."

"He followed me up here. I hope you don't mind?"

"If Blackie wants to be up here with you, there's nothing I can do to stop him. That's his nature," he smiled. "Miss Graham, I'm here to apologise for not having you join us at the supper table. My cousin thought you would want to get to know your young charges better. But from now on, I hope you will take all your meals with me. Annie can give the girls their evening bread and milk."

"Oh. Thank you, Mr Paterson."

"I trust you weren't offended."

"No. Of course not. I know governesses don't always eat with the family."

"They do at Leddrie Green. I suppose Alison told you I was once Bobby's tutor?"

"Yes, she did." Kirsty's small pink mouth opened in a smile, revealing attractive little teeth and for the first time he noticed how pretty she was. Her eyes were amber, like the cat's, and the dark hair hanging loose around her shoulders was thick and curly. "You mustn't worry about me, Mr Paterson. Though I'm afraid I did give you reason to think so, I don't take offence easily. And, I am so very glad to be here."

"I'm glad you're here too" he said, and meant it. With a courtly bow, he wished her goodnight and left.

In the library, Betsy had set out his manuscript together with her transcription. She seemed prepared to sit down and go over it with him but Walter told her he preferred to read it through by himself.

"You'll join me for a little nightcap later on?" she suggested. "And then we can talk about it?"

"If I finish it in time, Betsy, but please don't stay up for me. You have a long journey tomorrow." He ushered her firmly from the room and shut the door after her.

It was lucky that he had also given her time to go upstairs to the drawing room before he started to read.

She had completely rewritten his opening paragraph! Walter was furious. He had put deep thought over much time into finding the right order of words and her editing didn't strike him as any improvement. Worse was to come. She had changed his every sentence, cutting words out and substituting phrases of her own. He could never send this version to his editor. It wasn't his, and he didn't like it at all. Walter stood up and found the brandy Douglas had brought him. He drank a straight shot, then poured another, diluting it with water. He would be up all night, re-copying. And he had a right wrist which tired easily from an old injury. Around ten o'clock, Betsy knocked on the door and came in without waiting for a response. "Aren't you joining me for cocoa, Walter?"

He shook his head. He had taken off his coat and pulled his cravat loose. A small stack of fresh paper sat at one elbow. "No, thank you, Betsy. I don't want any cocoa tonight."

She looked down at the desk. "Did you like the way I revised your essays?"

He didn't know what to say.

"I really tightened up your prose, didn't I?"

"It undoubtedly need some pruning, but Betsy, I only asked you to copy the manuscript. Not edit it."

"You didn't agree with my changes?"

"Not all of them, I'm afraid. I appreciate what you tried to do, but it wasn't what I wanted. I'm sorry."

Her face fell. "You didn't like my version?"

"It wasn't what I wrote. . . That's why I'm having to copy it over again."

"You're re-copying it? Surely that's not necessary! Let us go over it together, I can explain my interpretation and . . ."

"I'm sure you can but there isn't time. I've too many

pages to transcribe by tomorrow morning. I don't mean to be ungrateful for your efforts or discourteous but please! Not now."

She began to cry.

Walter could never stand women in tears. His nerves were on edge and he felt the pressure of the task in front of him. He snapped; "For God's sake, Betsy! I have to finish this!" She buried her face in her hands and sobbed. He jumped up and shut the door so the servants wouldn't hear.

"Betsy, please!"

She threw herself at him, clung to him, her head on his shoulder and her arms around him. She wore a heady perfume he disliked.

"Betsy, control yourself. Please. I simply can't take this. . ." He managed to break away from her and retreated behind his chair. "I'm very sorry if I've upset you, but . . ." He stopped himself just in time before he told her what he really thought about her reworking of his meticulously constructed prose.

"Go to bed," he told her, trying to keep his voice pleasant. "We'll talk about it in the morning. After breakfast. There will be plenty of time before you leave." He took her by the arm and led her to the door. "Now goodnight. Sleep well."

He kissed her quickly and propelled her into the hall. Then he locked the door, refilled his glass, tried to compose himself. She was pounding on the woodwork, screaming.

"Stop that!" He called through the keyhole. "Please!" She redoubled her cries.

"Betsy!" He shouted back. "Be quiet! You'll waken the whole household! Do you want to embarrass yourself before the servants and Miss Graham?"

That silenced her. Next morning, she remained in her

bedroom, with a tray sent up, while Walter breakfasted with Kirsty and the children. He had finished the manuscript as dawn was breaking and had scarcely found time to shave and change his clothes. He was weary but intensely relieved. The tedious job of copying was behind him and it had been therapeutic to resume the work on his book. Moreover, he was pleased with the result. But now, willy-nilly, he would have to handle Betsy, and needed to do this in private.

"Miss Graham, it's a nice morning so why don't you walk down to the school with Mary and Anne and they'll introduce you to the dominie? Tell him you're going to be helping them with their homework." That would get her well away from the house.

"What a wonderful idea, Mr Paterson! Come along, girls!"

"Papa, why was Aunt Betsy making a scene last night?" asked Mary. "She was crying so loud she wakened me up."

"She . . . she was crying because she was worried about her mother. You'd better go in and say goodbye to her nicely before you leave for school. And be sure to thank her for all she's done for you."

"Is she coming back?" asked Anne.

"Sometime," said Walter vaguely. "Miss Graham, stay and observe the school for as long as you want. And when you return, I'd like you to meet Hannah the cook and discuss the meals with her. But talk with me first, if you please."

She smiled. "Very well. And I'd better make sure that Miss Paterson has some refreshment to take with her in the coach."

After they left, Walter wrapped up his manuscript, addressed it to his editor and took it round to the stables where the carriage was being readied for the trip to town.

"Rabb, I've some pages of a new book that I want you to deliver to my publisher. Don't say anything to Miss Paterson about it, please, because she might feel she should take care of it for me and she's going to be very busy. So put it in your own satchel and after you've taken her to Heriot Row, leave it at the publishing house. You know where that is, don't you?"

"Oh aye, sir. I took a package o' writing there once afore for ye."

Betsy was awaiting him in the hall, dressed for departure. Though her face showed traces of tears, she was once again her forceful self.

"I've packed all the clothes I'm leaving behind in big boxes," she informed him. "So if Miss Graham uses my room while I'm gone, they won't be in her way. Once I've seen how my mother is, I'll write and tell you when to expect me back here."

Walter took a deep breath. "Betsy. I think you should take your boxes with you."

"I won't need these dresses in the next few weeks."

"You'll need them eventually."

"But . . ."

"I want you to stay at home as long as you're needed. And, besides . . ." he braced himself. "Betsy, I am deeply grateful to you for all you have done for me. But, I know you prefer Edinburgh to the country and now someone is here to run the house and take care of the children, it's not necessary that you return."

To his horror, her eyes were filling again. "Walter, I . . ."

"I hope we will always be friends," he said. He couldn't put the unexpressed any more plainly.

Rabb had brought the carriage to the door and was tramping upstairs to collect her luggage.

"There are some boxes in the bedroom," Walter called after him. "Miss Paterson will tell you which ones to take. Betsy, go with him, if you please, and show him."

There was nothing else she could do. Sooner than he'd expected, Kirsty returned, her cheeks rosy from the fresh air. "The dominie wants to talk to me this afternoon when he has more leisure, Mr Paterson. So I'm picking the girls up after school and we're discussing their homework then."

"So maybe now you'd better go down to the kitchen," Walter told her. "To talk about meals with the cook. Miss Paterson hasn't had time. . ."

"Oh yes I have," said Betsy, descending upon them, Rabb in her wake. "I've written out menus for three weeks."

"Then you'd better make sure Hannah understands them, Miss Graham."

Taking the hint, Kirsty dipped a quick curtsy. "I wish you a pleasant journey, Miss Paterson." She disappeared, leaving the two cousins alone.

He started to escort Betsy to the carriage but she stopped him.

"There's something I must talk to you about, Walter. Can we go into the parlour and sit down for a moment?"

"If it concerns my manuscript, Betsy, I think it would be better if we simply left that subject closed. I know you meant well and I apologise if I was overly blunt last night."

"It isn't about that, Walter. And I know how sensitive authors are. You don't need to explain. But please! I do need to tell you something."

He followed her into the downstairs sitting room, leaving the door ajar. She was twisting her gloves, not looking at him. "Just before I came here to try to help you, Walter, an admirer of mine – Lord Munro, who just retired from the bench – asked me for my hand. His wife died last year. I told him I would have to think over his proposal, because you and your needs came first with me."

When he made no comment she continued. "Once I'm back in Edinburgh I will have to give him an answer. Tell him whether or not I will marry him."

Hope surged through Walter. "Oh but you must, Betsy! It would be a wonderful match. I remember Lord Munro. A brilliant man and he has a beautiful house in the New Town." Also old enough to be her father. "I'll come to your wedding and bring the girls."

Relief made him talkative. "I'm so glad you told me – shared your good news with me before you left. I'm sure you'll be very happy as Lady Munro. And now I mustn't keep you from your long journey. Congratulations and *bon voyage*, dear cousin."

Taking her arm he walked her quickly to the carriage, kissing her cheek fraternally, as he signalled to Rabb, who shook the horses' reins and started them cantering off down the drive.

With renewed energy, Walter ran downstairs to the kitchen. "Miss Graham. Hannah. I just wanted to suggest, could we have some plainer food? It's been too rich lately. I don't think it's good for the children."

The cook was beaming. "Oh aye, sir. I agree. All them fancy gravies. . . Miss Graham was just asking me if I remembered which of Mrs Paterson's recipes you especially liked, and I'm going to make . . ."

He held up his hand. "Surprise me!"

She bobbed a curtsy. "Beggin' your pardon for asking, sir, but . . . is Miss Paterson coming back?"

"No," he answered. "She isn't. She's going to be married in Edinburgh."

"I'm glad to hear it," said Hannah. "If ye'll excuse me for sayin' it, Mr Paterson, I didna think she was cut out for the country life. She wouldna gie me time to start the jam making, she was aye that concerned about the fricassees and Corstorphine Creams and fancy dishes. . ."

"Hannah's going to show me how she makes her special raspberry jelly," added Kirsty. Her sleeves were rolled up and she was tying an apron around her slim waist.

"Then I'd better make myself scarce. Men are in the way in a kitchen. And don't give me a big midday meal, please. Just a plate of plain broth."

"Very guid, sir," said Hannah, adding with the familiarity of the well established Scottish servant, "Annie telt me ye were up a' night writing. Maybe ye should gang upstairs and tak' a wee nap the now?"

He was touched. "I suppose I should but I don't feel tired. Later, maybe. But on this lovely sunny morning I want to go out and see how my crops are growing."

So for the first time since Primrose's death, the Leddrie Green household began to function smoothly. That Kirsty Graham was kin to the Laird's wife did her no harm with the servants and forewarned by Alison, she never gave direct orders. She appealed to them for information on how Walter liked things done, thanked them profusely for their advice and complimented them when they carried it out.

Walter had always noticed womens' clothes and as his interest in life began to revive under this gentle return to routine, he noticed that Kirsty had an extremely meagre wardrobe. Her only smart turnout was a well-cut riding habit. She was such an experienced horsewoman, he let her take the little girls out on their ponies whenever the weather permitted.

But her dresses were plain and out of style and when she changed for supper, she always wore the same dark dowdy maroon-coloured gown edged in black.

One evening, fortified by some wine, he said to her,

"Miss Graham, when I went to work for your cousin Alison, years ago, I had only one suit of clothes. So she passed on to me several garments that had belonged to her late husband."

Kirsty laughed. "They must have been far too wide for you, Mr Paterson! Cousin Robert was a fat man."

"Well, they had to be altered and never looked very fashionable, but I enjoyed wearing them, nonetheless." He smiled at the recollection. "When my wife was pregnant, I bought some lengths of silks in Glasgow so that she could order something new to wear, after she had borne the child. Alas, she never even knew about them. They were to be a surprise. So I have bolts of cloth in a library drawer doing no-one any good there."

"Could they be made up into dresses for the children?"

"No. The materials are too fragile and the colours aren't appropriate."

He refilled his glass and hers. She said nothing. She always waited, never interrupted his train of thought as Betsy had done. "I wonder, Miss Graham, would you like to look them over and pick out some you might fancy for yourself? There's a dressmaker in the village and I'll be glad to pay for her services."

Her amber eyes lit up. "Oh. How very thoughtful of you, Mr Paterson! I'm a good seamstress; I could make them up myself!"

"You've plenty to do without a lot of extra sewing. Let's go and see what we have."

Although she was different in complexion from his late wife, the colours suited her well, and her youthful delight, as she held up the lengths of material and draped them around her, was so infectious Walter enjoyed the evening instead of, as he had anticipated, suffering another trying experience. When they had had another glass of wine, he carried the silks upstairs to Betsy's vacated bedroom, where Kirsty was now well ensconced.

Happiness was slowing coming back into his home. In the evenings, he often had to close the library window while working on his book to shut out the noise of childish laughter in the garden. He was regaining his ability to write, encouraged by a favourable letter from his editor, and as he completed each new essay Kirsty copied it out, never changing a comma.

Sitting beside Walter and his daughters at church, she no longer looked mousy, for Alison had contributed shawls, gloves and refurbished bonnets to the new dresses. But if tongues were starting to wag in the parish, he didn't care. And, taking their cue from the Laird's wife, the gentry in the valley frequently included Miss Graham in their invitations to Walter to join them for supper or to play cards. It was an unusual sign of social acceptance for a governess.

VII

As the summer moved on, the people of Strathblane began to appreciate the reality of the Stewarts' departure for America. The doctor was much in Glasgow on emigration business and young Jock MacLean took over treating his patients, even the valetudinarian Henry Moncrieff.

In July, Jennifer Stewart – 'Auntie Jenny' to Angus and Tommy – joined her brother's family at Blaerisk. The Reverend Mr Stewart planned to remarry, although to which of several widows in his parish was not yet a certainty, according to his disgusted daughter. Jean's pregnancy was advancing and Jenny made herself useful packing furnishings and household linens. She hoped to find employment in America as a governess or housekeeper and struck up a warm friendship with Kirsty Graham, who often visited the Stewart household with Walter.

On the Sunday before the family were due to sail from Port Glasgow, Mr Gardner asked the doctor to act as precentor at the morning service and let him pick the hymns. Douglas led the congregation in his favourite excerpt from Haydn's *Creation*, then in the Twenty-third Psalm to the tune of *Crimond*. The venerable Strathblane church was in process of being rebuilt and full of dust and piles of masonry but everyone had brought stools and chairs and after the benediction, the villagers made no move to rise and depart. The Laird moved up to the front and faced them.

"Mrs Stewart, please come and stand beside me and your husband too," he requested, and when they did so, Henry Moncrieff handed Jean a heavy leather-bound book and a thick purse. "These gifts," he said, "are from the people of Strathblane. The Bible is for your family. And since we collected more money than was needed to buy it, we are giving it to you for the doctor undoubtedly has a few uncollected bills. Here it is, Mrs Stewart. I know you have always kept his accounts."

Jean shook her head. "He earned it. . ." She passed the bag to her husband, who opened it. "Dougie. . . Say something," she prompted.

Douglas was so deeply moved, he had to clear his throat several times before he could speak.

"The last time I sang the Twenty-third Psalm," he said finally, "was in my father's kirk in Darnick. And, as I stood up to precent this morn, I minded that day and how there were no known faces in his congregation. And here I knew everyone – and no to speak it carnally, some o' ye inside as well as out." They smiled.

"When I got my degree from the Edinburgh Medical College," he continued, "my ambition was to be a fashionable city physician rather than a country doctor. I arrived in Strathblane a disappointed, bitter man and no one will ever know how lonely. In the Blane Valley I found a wonderful wife, a fine young colleague in whose hands now I leave your health, and many good friends." His eyes lingered on Walter and Mr Gardner. "And, for the rest of ye, we've had our flytings and arguments over the years, but when I move across the sea to that country I'm told I must call the United States, not simply America, I want ye to know that I'll look back on ye all and I'll be remembering ye with . . . with deep appreciation and love."

He sat down quickly, pulled out a clean white handkerchief and unabashedly dried his eyes.

Jean stepped forward. "I've aye wanted a family Bible," she said. "And I'll sit down wi this one the day and write out on its first page the date of my marriage to Douglas Stewart, and when a' our children were born, e'en that wee dead one that lies out there in the kirkyard alangside ma faither and mother and a' ma forebears." Tears ran down her cheeks. "Thank ye all. It's sair for me to leave Strathblane, but I've aye tried to follow the word o' this Guid Book." She turned to her husband. "And so like Ruth, amid the alien corn, I'm saying *Whither thou goest I will go.*"

The whole parish turned out to see the Stewarts off next morning, even the Laird and Mrs Moncrieff with their young family. Schoolchildren filled Jean's arms with posies of wild flowers. There were many little gifts and packages of food to eat on the way. Their furniture and baggage had already been sent ahead to Port Glasgow and they were travelling in the Leddrie Green carriage, as they had done on their trip to Darnick, but this time Walter was escorting them on horseback and he was not alone.

"Mr Paterson," Kirsty had said at supper on Sunday night, "please may I come with you tomorrow? On horseback, I mean. There's no room in the carriage."

"It's a lengthy journey, Miss Graham. Much further than into the city."

"I'm used to long rides, growing up on Loch Lomondside, and I enjoy them. Please! The girls are spending the day with their little cousins at Kirklands because there's no school. The dominie declared a holiday. He knew none of the children could think about lessons with the Stewarts leaving and everyone so sad about it."

"How sensible of him, and I'm glad the Kirk Session gave him permission."

"So I'd be free to go with you, Mr Paterson and I've never been *doon the wa'er* as they say."

"And it's beautiful country. I planned to travel home in the coach, with Rabb leading my horse. I suppose he could handle two just as easily as one." The prospect of company for the sad journey was attractive. "Yes. You can come with me. You'll enjoy seeing the countryside and it looks as though it'll be a good day."

So next morning, when the carriage finally started lumbering up the hill, the villagers waving and calling out farewells, Walter and Kirsty on their respective mounts rode alongside, as escorts.

At the top of the brae, before starting the descent towards the Valley of the Clyde, Douglas called to Rabb to stop. Jean got out of the carriage slowly because of her pregnancy and looked for the last time at the Campsie Fells. It was a clear day and she could see Ben Lomond, the first of the Highland mountains to the north, in the background. Tears poured down her cheeks, but after clasping her hands as if in silent prayer, she turned and got back in beside her husband and children. Walter and Kirsty, deeply moved, cantered on ahead. He kept his mind off the imminent parting by pointing out landmarks to her. When the excited little Stewarts demanded, and got, a stop for a 'picnic', the two equestrians joined them.

The doctor was unusually silent, the magnitude of the step he was taking heavy upon him. Jean could not staunch her tears. None of the adults could eat, although Rabb reminded them that they had better get some nourishment before starting their choppy voyage. The children chattered. Angus was full of plans on how he would impress the Americans. Tommy was worrying about his favourite dog which he had left behind with Anne Paterson.

Fortunately, the good weather held and the exercise raised Walter's spirits. Kirsty concentrated on her horsemanship which she obviously enjoyed and galloping ahead, they arrived in Port Glasgow in time to tether their mounts at the inn and walk down to the waterside before the carriage caught up with them.

Jean's cousin, Willie MacDougal was already there to supervise his vessel's departure and his wife was with him. "Yon's the ship." He pointed with pride to a dark heavy freighter tied alongside the dock. "She'll no be sailing for a while, for there's more cargo to load. Forby we hae to wait for the tide to turn." He addressed the family. "Ye'd best take the bairns aboard and settle in afore she goes. So make yer farewells the now."

Jean threw her arms around Walter. "Oh ma dearie, take care o' yersel. . ."

"*Et toi aussi.*" He tried to smile. "You remember I always lapse into French when . . . when . . ."

With streaming eyes, she kissed Mrs MacDougal and her cousin Willie, who gestured to a seaman to help her up the gangplank. Jenny and the children followed in her wake. The expression on her husband's face as he stepped out of the carriage and saw the ship stirred Walter's memory of the aristocrats in Paris en route to the guillotine.

"You're not mounting a tumbril, *mon brave*," he reassured his old friend, "you're beginning a new career. A rebirth!"

"Aye. . . but birth is aye painful."

"Here's a thing to ease that pain, doctor," said Rabb, handing over a dark bottle. "Genuine Strathblane whisky to remember us by. Guid for the seasickness."

"Illegally distilled, I hope?" said Douglas, forcing a smile.

"Oh, aye."

"Thank you. I'll take it when the going is rough." He shook hands with the coachman then turned to the shipowner who pronounced with his usual bluntness, "Ye'll be afloat lang enough to get over the sickness and find yer sea legs, Dougie. Be sure ye send me a full report on how to keep ma crews healthy."

"Aye right, Willie. I'll be a good ship's surgeon. And keep in touch wi Jean . . . she'll miss her relatives. . ."

He threw his arms around Walter. "And you, laddie, take care o' yersel. . ."

"*Bon chance! Bon voyage, mon brave! Écrivez!* Come back and visit when you're rich and famous!"

"I'll never be either, Paterson."

"Oh yes you will! You have the chance, now . . . a new life!"

Douglas stepped back, gave his friend a long clinical look. "*You're* gestatin' new life, too. And I'm thankful to see ye start to heal before I go." He glanced towards Kirsty. "And now . . . as they say . . ." He held up the whisky. "*Here's tae us! Wha's like us? Damn' few and they're a' deid.*"

He stumbled up the gangplank after his family.

"Ye've time to gang to the pub and hae a meal, Mr Paterson," said Willie MacDougal. "Unless you and your lady would like to see over the ship?"

Walter shook his head. "No thank you, Mr Mac-Dougal. Since I landed in Scotland from France ten years ago, I've never set foot on another boat. And Miss Graham should have some refreshment. Perhaps someone would let us know when . . . when the departure is imminent?"

"I'll do that for you, sir" said Rabb.

At the ordinary Kirsty, with youthful appetite, ate a great platterful of lamb and turnips. Walter drank brandy. It was the lowest moment of his life since his wife's death. Douglas and Jean had been a second family to him, as close to his heart as his parents and sister in Edinburgh. He knew he would never see the Stewarts again. They would not come back to Scotland. They would write letters, of course, but the friendship would not be the same.

Rabb came by to say that the ship was about to sail, but when they hastened down to the dockside, the vessel had already cast off. They could only cry, "*Bon voyage!*" to Douglas, Jean, Jenny and the children, all at the rails waving and calling out last minute messages. The only one Walter heard clearly was little Tommy's tearful cry, "Mr Paterson, tell Anne to tak' care o' ma doggie!"

Then, for better or worse, they were gone.

The heavy freighter drifted out into the channel, the wind caught the sails, a beautiful and impressive sight, and she swept smoothly beyond reach of the land.

Willie MacDougal, with a grunt, departed for his Glasgow office in a small trap, taking his wife along with him. Rabb encouraged Walter and Kirsty into the carriage.

"There's no sense in hanging around here, sir," he explained. "It's a fair journey back to Strathblane. And we canna hurry when I'm leadin' yer two mounts."

Walter was so emotionally and physically exhausted, and had drunk so much brandy on an empty stomach, he fell asleep almost as soon as they left Port Glasgow.

He dosed on, lulled by the motion of the carriage and when he eventually woke and looked out the window, he could see Ben Lomond in the distance and the Campsie Fells on the immediate horizon.

But even the sight of his beloved Blane Valley could not fill the terrible void in his soul. Primrose, Jean, Douglas Stewart . . . they were all gone now and he was alone. But was he? Not physically at least, for a warm somnolent female body leaned trustfully against his side. Kirsty had taken off her hat and her dark hair tumbled around her little face, making it appear unusually white. The tip of her nose was pink from wind and tears, but her lips turned up in a secret smile. She looks exactly like Blackie, thought Walter fondly.

But cats had no smell and Kirsty's body gave off an agreeable aroma of healthy young femininity intermingled with horse. Walter, to his astonishment, found it embarrassingly erotic.

In the shock of his wife's death, he had believed himself impotent, although when he mentioned this to the doctor, Douglas had laughed and told him in earthy language that under the proper stimulus performance would return.

"And if you're nervous about it, Paterson, the treatment according to one of my Edinburgh colleagues is to lie with an attractive woman all night but restrain yourself from letting your lust get the upper hand. That restores confidence and on the next occasion all is well."

He was pondering the relevance of this in his proximity to Kirsty when she stirred, stretched with feline grace and opened amber eyes outlined by black lashes.

"Oh, I beg your pardon, Mr Paterson! I didn't mean to crowd you!" She made to draw away, but he slipped his arm around her and when he pressed her to him, she offered no resistance.

"Do you know that you have a little cat's face, Miss Graham?"

"My father used to say that. He always called me Kitty."

"May I call you Kitty too?"

"Yes, please. Where are we?"

"At the top of the Mugdock Brae, heading for Strathblane."

"Nearly home," she said drowsily.

"Kitty. Are you happy at Leddrie Green?"

"Oh yes, Mr Paterson," she yawned. "Very happy. I hope I'll be there a long time with you and the children."

He thought of Douglas Stewart's last comment, and suddenly realized what he should do. "Kitten, how old are you?"

"I'm twenty."

"There's something I want to talk to you about and it's important so you must listen carefully."

"I'll try, Mr Paterson. Oh dear! I hope I haven't done something to displease you?"

"No, indeed. Christina. Kirsty. Kitten. I'm twelve years older than you. And although I live comfortably, I will never be a rich man or even a famous literary one. I am no catch for a young lady who's as pretty as you are."

She raised her eyes to his and sat very still.

"I was so lonely before you came into my life, I don't want to lose you. Would you consider settling permanently in my household?"

Her whole body shivered with joy. "Oh. Oh. Mr Paterson. Do you mean that?"

"Yes. I do. I'm offering you my hand in marriage. But you mustn't do anything hasty that you might regret.

You don't need to give me an answer now. Think about what a union between us could mean. Talk it over with Alison or with your mother or . . . whoever."

"I don't need to do that," said Kirsty. "I make my own decisions. I always have. I accept your offer, Mr Paterson."

His heart was beating furiously. It was too good to be true. "But you mustn't be impulsive."

"I am never impulsive, Mr Paterson."

"Please! My name is Walter. And I don't want you to be in a hurry, to do something you might feel differently about later on."

"But I won't."

"How can you be so sure? You've just had a long tiring day. You may not be thinking clearly."

"Mr Paterson. Walter. I *am* thinking clearly. I fell in love with you before I ever met you. When I read your books . . . such original, sensitive portraits of country life! And your beautiful poetry. . . And then I saw you and I was even more in love with you. When you didn't want me in your house, I was terribly hurt."

"You . . . fell in love with me?"

"Yes. That very first day Alison took me over to Leddrie Green."

"When I treated you like a boor?"

"No, you didn't Mr Pa . . . Walter. You were just canny. And, and please! I don't want to, to scare you. I don't expect you to feel as I do. I know that . . . that this is just an arrangement. You want me to run your household and . . ."

"Oh no! I want a lot more than that!"

"So do I," said Kirsty frankly and put her arms around him, her lips meeting his.

They were so amorously intertwined when they drew

up in front of Leddrie Green House that Rabb spent some time coughing loudly before he opened the carriage door and set down the steps for them to alight. The servants were all waiting up for them and Hannah had prepared a hot filling soup and a platterful of cold meats.

"It's late," Walter said to Annie, as she served these. "So tomorrow morning, I don't want you to bring up my shaving water or serve breakfast until I ring. And Miss Graham will also be tired. She should sleep late, so don't disturb her either. Just dress the children as you always do, see they eat their porridge and send them off to school. Now go to bed, yourself, it's very late and please thank Hannah for the nice supper."

At the door of the master bedroom, he took Kirsty in his arms again. "After what we've decided . . . do you really want to sleep next door tonight?"

She laughed quietly. "No. But . . . it wouldn't be proper, would it?"

"Do you care about propriety?"

"I care about what you think of me."

"I think it mightn't be proper but it would be very nice and why not?"

"I'm . . . a virgin, Mr Pa . . . Walter . . . "

"Don't be scared. So was Primrose. I'll be gentle, I promise you."

"But wouldn't you think the less of me if I disregarded marriage vows?"

"How can you disregard vows you have not yet made? But if you are afraid I won't marry you once I've . . . enjoyed you as they say, how can I convince you that I'm serious about our marriage? I swear before God that I am. Maybe I don't love you in the way I loved Primrose but I am sure that will come."

He tilted up her face, kissed her again, then drew off

his signet ring and guided it onto her finger. "Kitten, this pledged my troth to my first wife. Let it do the same to my second." When she still hesitated, he went on, "If you wish, I will call to Annie and Hannah to come up here and I'll declare my intentions in their presence. That would marry us legally in Scotland, as I am sure you well know."

He reached for a little bell on the landing table but before he could ring it, she covered his hands with hers. "No, Walter. I love you and I trust you."

She pushed open his bedroom door. After he had overcome her first strangeness and fear, he was amazed by her frank passion for his body and relieved that it aroused similar emotion in his own flesh. When they were satisfied, she cuddled beside him, her fingers like a cat's paws kneading his bare chest.

They slept far into the morning. Eventually he got up and very quietly opened his door to find that Annie had left two trays with fruit, scones, butter, honey and jam, outside their respective doors. Their water jugs for washing were by now stone cold.

They ate breakfast in bed and when they had finished, he said, "The first thing I have to do today, if I ever get up! is go and talk to Mr Gardner. Do you want an elegant *penny wedding*?"

"I don't care what kind of wedding we have. But I do think, dear Walter, that it had better be soon. . . "

"Then let us have a quiet ceremony, with just the necessary witnesses. Your cousin Alison perhaps, and the Laird?"

She giggled. "That might make us respectable. But we can't be married before next week."

"Why not?"

"The banns have to be cried in the kirk. I'm a minister's daughter, I know about these things. So my mother and my sisters could come over from Tarbet. That would certainly make us respectable."

"Why are you worried about our respectability?"

She beamed at him, licking honey off her fingers. "I'm very much afraid, dear Walter, that however you try to pull the wool over the servants' eyes, what happened last night will be all over the parish before the end of the day."

"*Dieu!* You're probably right." He struck his forehead in mock horror. "Maybe we'd better elope and stay away from Strathblane until the scandal dies down. We could go to Edinburgh and take our vows before my uncle the judge. You'd meet my family and go shopping with Clemmie." He was genuinely distressed. "Kitten, I'm shattered! Truly, I didn't mean to destroy your reputation."

"You didn't," she said smiling. "I had no choice. You exercised *le droit de seigneur.*"

Walter started to laugh and laugh as though he couldn't stop.

"What is it?" she asked, a little scared. "Whatever did I say?"

"*Plus ça change, plus c'est la meme chose!* Here I thought I was a good, modern, Nineteenth Century man who had moved with the times and put the *Ancien Regime* and all its wickedness behind me!"

She held up her left hand. "Well, you did put your ring on my finger first."